FROM THE
COURTROOM
OF HEAVEN

TO THE THRONE OF
GRACE AND MERCY

REVISED AND EXPANDED

JEANETTE STRAUSS

2011 © Jeanette Strauss

This book is protected under the copyright laws of the United States of America. All rights reserved. This book may not be copied or reprinted for commercial gain or profit. The use of short quotations or occasional page copying for personal or group study is permitted and encouraged. Permission will be granted upon request.

Unless otherwise noted, scriptures are from the New King James Version Bible. Copyright 1982 by Thomas Nelson, Inc. Used by permission.

Scriptures marked AMP are from the Amplified® Bible, Copyright © 1954, 1958, 1962, 1964, 1965, 1987 by The Lockman Foundation. Used by permission.

Scriptures marked NIV are taken from THE HOLY BIBLE, NEW INTERNATIONAL VERSION®, NIV® Copyright © 1973, 1978, 1984, 2011 by Biblica, Inc.™ Used by permission. All rights reserved worldwide

Text marked (Commentary) is commentary taken from the New Spirit-Filled Life Bible, Copyright 2002 by Thomas Nelson, Inc. Used by permission.

Please note that the name "satan" and all names related to him are not capitalized. I have made a conscious decision not to capitalize his name, even to the point of violating grammar rules.

Published by Glorious Creations Publications: www.gloriouscreations.net

ISBN: 978-0-9907742-4-2
Cover art by James Nesbit of Prepare the Way Ministries, International www.ptwministries.com

Table of Contents

	INTRODUCTION	I
	A WORD FROM JEANETTE	II
1	THE REVELATION OF THE COURTROOM	1
2	THE COURTROOM IN A BELIEVER'S LIFE	5
3	THE DREAM	11
4	DREAM COME TRUE	19
5	DREAM INTERPRETATION	21
6	THE JUDGE	29
7	THE PROSECUTOR	43
8	THE AMBASSADOR OF RECONCILIATION	61
9	DEFENSE ATTORNEY — OUR ADVOCATE	75
10	SECRET WEAPON AGAINST THE ACCUSER	77
11	THE BATTLE IS GOD'S!	83
12	VICTIM OR VICTOR?	89
13	INTERCESSION OR SPIRITUAL WARFARE?	97
14	FOR THE BACKSLIDDEN OR UNSAVED	103
15	ADDRESSING THE ACCUSER	109
16	PRAISES	111
17	REPENT, REPENT, PETITION, PRAISE	113
	ABOUT THE AUTHOR	117

Introduction

A Believer's Handbook for Legislating from the Heavenlies

In answer to a prayer for our daughter, I had a dream. In the dream, I found myself in a heavenly Courtroom standing before the Judge of heaven and earth. He explained why my husband and I hadn't received answers to our prayers sooner, and instructed us to pray in a specific way. After following the Courtroom protocol, He revealed to me, our prayers were answered within one week—after seven years of praying in every other way we knew how to pray.

As we follow the directions of the Lord, we can be assured of the victory. This doesn't mean every outcome will be what you expected, but the outcome will be the Lord's will for each situation. The Judge of heaven and earth is inviting you to appear in His Courtroom.

"I, even I, am He who blots out your transgressions for My own sake; And I will not remember your sins. Put Me in remembrance; Let us contend together; State your case, that you may be acquitted. —Isaiah 43:25-26

As believers, our purpose in the Courtroom of Heaven is to make intercession as an Ambassador of Reconciliation, to stand in the gap on behalf of people, regions, governments, and nations.

Let us therefore come boldly to the throne of grace, that we may obtain mercy and find grace to help in time of need.
—Hebrews 4:16

With Jesus as our Redeemer, the Word as our Defense, the Holy Spirit as our Counselor, and the Judge as our Father, we can win our case in heaven's Courtroom for victory on the earth.

A Word from Jeanette

After sharing and teaching on the subject of "From the Courtroom of Heaven to the Throne of Grace and Mercy" for several years, it seemed necessary to revise the book to include additional scriptures and revelations that I have received as I helped people make their appearance in the Courtroom of Heaven.

I would like to share one of my revelatory experiences with you. While preparing to speak to a women's home prayer group about the Courtroom of Heaven, I had the most amazing experience.

I stood in front of the fireplace, facing a home full of women waiting expectantly for the meeting to start. They were visiting with each other as they found their seats. I could see the living room, dining room and kitchen because it was an open floor plan. It seemed that every space was filled, all the way to the back door. There were at least 50 women gathered in that space and I wasn't sure that everyone would have a seat.

I noticed that there was a large overstuffed comfortable looking chair to my left. I was about to say something like; "There is a chair up here if someone would like it." Before I could say anything, I saw the back door open (with my spiritual eyes) and I saw Jesus come walking through that door into the house!

He made His way toward me, walking purposely around and through the women. He was reaching out and touching people as He came, but looking at me all the while, and I was looking at Him. It was if our eyes were locked onto each other. I had never had anything like this happen before, so all I could do was watch Him with my heart racing, and wondering what He was going to do. I was questioning what I was seeing.

He walked right up to that chair off to my left and sat down. He was smiling at me. Just then, the leader called the meeting to order and asked if I would pray an opening prayer. I said I would, while wondering to myself, "How am I going to do this?" I was feeling quite undone.

I began to pray with words coming out of my mouth, but my mind was addressing Jesus. I asked Him, "Jesus is there something you want me to share or do differently in this meeting?" I had my head bowed and my eyes closed as I prayed. I heard Him answer me in my spirit. He said; "I have come to hear you share with these ladies about My book of love."

I thought, "He means the Bible, and He is pleased with all of the scriptures I have in this book to validate the Courtroom in Heaven." As soon as that thought crossed my mind, He corrected me. He said; "I am talking about the Courtroom of Heaven book. It is My book of love given to help My children who I love very much. It brings me great joy when My children win their battles."

As I finished the verbal prayer, I hoped it made sense. Just in case it didn't, I decided to share what I had seen as a testimony of encouragement. They were so excited; the air of expectancy was suddenly as high as the heavens in that room, it was as if the roof had been blown off!

When I finished with the testimony, the leader came up and took the microphone. She began to share that at every meeting they always left an empty chair by whoever was speaking. This chair was designated for Jesus to sit in and they all knew it! This was the first time someone had shared that they had seen Jesus come in and sit down. This confirmed to them that the Lord was present, and not only had He heard, but acted on their prayers! He was sitting in the chair and now they had an actual "sighting."

I know some of you are thinking, "Were people supernaturally healed as Jesus brushed against them?" Many testimonies have come from that group. These women have become dear sisters to me. I usually share with them about once a year, so I get a lot of feedback. God has done many wonderful and miraculous things among them, as they have used the Courtroom of Heaven strategies found in the book.

So when you read this book and share it with others, you can be assured that Jesus is present and smiling, because this book isn't just about a Judge and the law, but about the love of our Father God towards us—His children. He is teaching us and training us to walk daily in the "Favor of God" so that we may receive all the blessings He has for us.

This revised version of the book includes additional revelation and scriptures the Lord has revealed to me, along with more testimonies from those who have won their cases in the Courtroom of Heaven. I hope you enjoy this revised and expanded version.

Blessings,

Jeanette

Chapter One

The Revelation Of the Courtroom

As citizens of God's kingdom, our goal is to bring heaven to earth and establish His rule.

"Your kingdom come, your will be done, on earth as it is in Heaven." —Matthew 6:10

There are strategies found in the Word that will bring His rule to the earth. One of those strategies is to appear before the Judge who rules the universe from the unseen Courtroom of Heaven. This book is about kingdom of heaven intercession. The Word teaches us the correct protocol for presenting a case in His Courtroom, and how to win that case.

The eligibility to present a case in the Courtroom of Heaven is reserved for the select group of people called believers. Jesus reaffirms this.

Jesus said to him, "I am the way, the truth, and the life. No one comes to the father except through me." —John 14:6

We are not limited in the type or number of cases we can present. As Ambassadors of Reconciliation, the Lord desires that we, as His children, bring every person we know into this Courtroom and make an appeal on their behalf. It doesn't matter if they are saved yet or not. It will be much better to get them into the

Courtroom in intercession now, while they are alive, than to take the chance that the only time they will appear before the Judge is on Judgment Day where there is no second chance.

Every soul is important to the Lord. Each person has a purpose to fulfill that no one else can accomplish. This divine destiny was chosen for him or her before they were in their mother's womb.

Before I formed you in the womb I knew you; before you were born I set you apart. I appointed you a prophet to the nations. —Jeremiah 1:5 NIV

And He has made from one blood every nation of men to dwell on the face of the earth, and has determined their pre-appointed times and the boundaries of their dwellings.
—Acts 17:26

If the enemy is able to capture these souls through sin in their lives, it will be impossible for them to accomplish the purpose the Lord has planned for them. There may be some success in their lives that brings a measure of satisfaction, but it will be worth nothing if the work hasn't been led of the Lord Jesus Christ. All their hard work will be burned up in the end. To make matters worse, it will lead to eternal torment. We have to help them! The Lord hates the sin that binds people, but loves the person and longs to see them set free.

For the son of man has come to seek and to save that which was lost. —Luke 19:10

You may identify with the Courtroom as a strategy you have already been using in your prayers. Hopefully there will be some additional revelation that will be helpful. I am not discounting the many other ways to pray, nor am I saying that this is a sure-fire method that will bring immediate results. God has His time and seasons in every situation.

As we follow His directions, we can be assured of the victory. This does not mean every outcome will be what you expected, but the outcome will be the Lord's will for each situation. Once the case is settled in the Courtroom in Heaven, it is settled on the earth. We can rest peacefully in that knowledge.

The following chapters are dedicated to explaining the workings of this Courtroom. You will be introduced to the various participants that are found in the Courtroom and the protocol required, if you are to take an active part in this most exciting opportunity.

Blessed is the man you choose, and cause to approach you, that he may dwell in Your courts, we shall be satisfied with the goodness of your house, of your holy temple.
Psalm 65:4

Chapter Two

The Courtroom In A Believer's Life

As a born-again Christian, I had never given much thought to the Courtroom of Heaven or the scriptures that speak of the Righteous Judge. Then I had a dream where the Lord instructed me to make an appearance in His Courtroom.

Before my life-changing dream, I realized that I believed the Judgment coming from the Righteous Judge would be against those who didn't believe in Jesus. I thought that unbelievers, after they died, would find themselves before The Great White Throne of Judgment, which is the final judgment spoken of in the book of Revelation. After this, unbelievers would go on to eternal punishment. I didn't know about the heavenly Courtroom that is always in session.

When I speak of the Courtroom of Heaven I am not referring to the Great White Throne of Judgment. I am speaking of another throne of judgment located in a heavenly Courtroom. There is no shortage of scriptures that reference this heavenly Courtroom.

In this Court, the Lord is willing to let His people bring Him any grievances they may have with the way the enemy has treated them.

Oh Lord, You have pleaded the case for my soul; You have redeemed my life. O Lord, You have seen how I am wronged; Judge my case. —Lamentations 3:58-59

Then hear in heaven, and act, and judge Your servants, condemning the wicked, bringing his way on his head, and justifying the righteous by giving him according to his righteousness. —1 Kings 8:32

I didn't have an understanding that, as we go through various trials in this life, these same trials are being played out in a Courtroom before the Judge of heaven and earth. Testimony concerning believers is heard. Decisions are being made that affect our lives, depending on the verdict rendered by the Righteous Judge, according to the Law, which is His Word.

As intercessors, we can bring situations into the heavenly Courtroom for resolution. The opportunity to appear and defend ourselves in this Courtroom is a privilege and honor that is available to every believer. The opportunity to appear as an intercessor is also welcomed by the Judge, but not by the prosecuting attorney.

Blessed is the man you choose, and cause to approach you, That he may dwell in Your courts, we shall be satisfied with the goodness of your house, of your holy temple. —Psalm 65:4

We can come into God's Courtroom and know we will be heard because our sins have been paid for through the shed blood of Jesus on the cross at Calvary. His blood has the power to wash our sins away. As we live our life on earth, we sometimes stumble and fall into sin. No man is capable of living a perfect sinless life; only Jesus did that. When we sin, we need to humble ourselves before the Lord, repent and ask forgiveness, so that we can be restored to fellowship with Him.

An 'end of days' deception

I think it is important to bring clarity to an issue that the body of Christ is struggling with right now.

There is a disturbing teaching that says once we are saved, we are under grace and can enjoy a free "all expense paid life." This teaching goes on to say that God is not judging believers in this lifetime; He is only judging the demonic. The teaching also says a person who commits sin and doesn't repent will suffer consequences, but not the judgment of God.

I have heard it said; "We aren't living under the law but under grace." Paul addresses this subject when writing to New Testament believers in Rome.

> *For sin shall not [any longer] exert dominion over you, since now you are not under Law [as slaves], but under grace [as subjects of God's favor and mercy]. What then [are we to conclude]? Shall we sin because we live not under Law but under God's favor and mercy? Certainly not! Do you not know that if you continually surrender yourselves to anyone to do his will, you are the slaves of him whom you obey, whether that be to sin, which leads to death, or to obedience which leads to righteousness (right doing and right standing with God)?* —Romans 6:14–15 AMP

Sin will place a believer in bondage. We are free from bondage as long as we repent for our sins, receive forgiveness, and are obedient to the Word. This doesn't mean we have freedom from problems in life or that we won't have to sacrifice our own will to the will of God.

We must be on our guard for any teaching that doesn't agree with the Word of God, no matter how anointed the minister. We will each stand before God and have to answer for ourselves. We can't try to cast blame for sin in our lives on someone else.

We are warned in the last days not to become one who wants to hear things that make us feel good but are not backed by the Word of God. In 2 Timothy, Paul warns that men will not want to hear sound doctrine.

For the time will come when they will not endure sound doctrine, but according to their own desires, because they have itching ears, they will heap up for themselves teachers; and they will turn their ears away from the truth, and be turned aside to fables. But you be watchful in all things, endure afflictions, do the work of an evangelist, fulfill your ministry. —2 Timothy 4:3-5

They want to do what they want to do. They will turn away from the truth to fables, which are stories that sound good but aren't the truth.

And Jesus answering them began to say, Take heed lest any man deceive you. —Mark 13:5

We live under God's grace as long as we are obedient to the laws of the kingdom of heaven. The Lord has extended His grace and mercy to us, but as the Word says, we can remove ourselves from this grace through various sins.

If we want to do our own thing but it doesn't agree with the Word of God, the Word is clear that we open a door for the enemy and we move ourselves out from under grace and become slaves once again to sin.

Jesus answered them, I assure you, most solemnly I tell you, whoever commits and practices sin is the slave of sin. —John 8:34 AMP

Do not be deceived, God is not mocked; for whatever a man sows, that he will also reap. —Galatians 6:7

New believers, and sometimes old believers, need to be encouraged to believe that they can overcome their temptations and live a victorious life.

We should run to the Courtroom every time the Holy Spirit convicts us of sin. We have access to this Courtroom 24/7, 365 days a year. This Courtroom is never closed to us, nor are we limited as to the number of cases we can bring before our Creator.

If you are in a crisis or have concerns over something or someone, take it to the Courtroom. By presenting the case to the Righteous Judge, you will be free from the burden. He is familiar with every case already; He won't be surprised at anything. He knows the truth because nothing is hidden from Him, and he knows the best way to resolve the case. No matter how impossible the case might seem to you, He won't turn it down. In fact, the more impossible it seems, the more He gets the glory.

Children, obey your parents in the Lord, for this is right. "Honor your father and mother," which is the first commandment with promise: "that it may be well with you and you may live long on the earth."
Ephesians 6:1-3

Chapter Three

The Dream

After seven years of praying for our daughter Stacie's backslidden spiritual condition, my husband, Bud, and I had become discouraged and frustrated. She was a born-again, Bible believing Christian who had gradually faded away from her Christian values and way of life.

Even if a Christian is not walking with the Lord, they probably know that what they are doing is wrong. They may still confess Jesus as their Savior, but they don't very often attend church or read the Word because it literally convicts them of their sins.

They move themselves out of the kingdom of light where the Lord is King, into the kingdom of darkness where satan rules and enslaves. This was the case with our daughter. We prayed every way we knew how to pray. We pleaded and decreed scripture to the Lord. We addressed the enemy; we commanded and demanded the release of our daughter. We bound satan up in the name of Jesus. We claimed the blood of Jesus over her. We did this for years without any visible results. We felt like we were fighting a losing battle.

We weren't prepared for the test this would turn out to be for us. We thought we had done most everything right in raising her, but at times we blamed ourselves for her backslidden state. We have found that this is common in Christian families. Parents have done their best to raise the child properly, but the child chooses to go the way of the world. We know that children have to find their own way, which can be a heartrending time for the parents.

For Stacie's sake, we wish it wouldn't have happened, but the Lord was faithful to her. He brought her back as He promised us in His Word He would do. He will be faithful in your situation too.

One night while we were praying for her, out of frustration and some fear I admit, we asked the Lord for a new strategy for prayer for her. I think the Lord was waiting for that prayer because He answered it that very night. This is the account of the dream that followed our prayer.

In the dream, Stacie and I were standing in a long, wide hallway. She asked me if I would help her. I told her I would and asked what she needed. She pointed to a door in the hallway and asked if I would go in and get her things that were in the room. She said she couldn't go into the room because someone was watching the room and, if they saw her, they would catch her and kill her.

I walked over to the door, opened it a crack and looked in. I saw a small, dimly lit room. Directly across from the door, on the other side of the room, there was a large window that was letting in muted light. I saw only one piece of furniture: a bed that took up most of the room. The clothes she had asked me to get were scattered all over the bed. On the other side of the window I could see people standing around with beer bottles in their hands, smoking and laughing. I could hear loud music. It appeared to be a worldly party scene.

I opened the door a little wider and slid through the opening. I began to gather up her clothing, and as I was doing this I kept glancing at the window. There was a person on the other side of the window standing with his back to the window. He was talking with several others.

He must have sensed something was going on behind him because he suddenly turned around and looked into the room directly at me. I could see that he was surprised. As our eyes locked, he stepped right through the glass of the window and was instantly standing in front of me. This person (spirit) placed a hand on either side of my face and began to twist my head. I knew his intention was to break my neck to kill me. I raised my hands up and knocked his hands loose but he grabbed my hands and held them together in front of me, placing me in a position of helplessness.

I heard these words echoing loudly through my mind, spoken by the Holy Spirit, "Your daughter is a lawful captive of the enemy. Her case is in My Court. Stand in the gap and repent on behalf of sin committed against Me by her and ask My forgiveness for the sin. Petition Me, the Righteous Judge of Heaven and Earth, to move her case from the Courtroom of Judgment into the Throne Room of Grace and Mercy. Ask for a season of grace on her life and I will remove the veil from the eyes of her understanding and show her the truth."

Then I heard more words vibrate loudly within my inner man. The voice said, "Isaiah 49:24 and 25." These last words woke me up. My mind was rapidly trying to process what had just occurred. I ran through the dream in my mind, preparing to go into this spiritual Courtroom as the dream had instructed me. It occurred to me that before I went into the Courtroom of Heaven on anyone's behalf, I had better be spiritually clean before the Judge myself.

Our own sin can be used as a technicality that causes us to lose the case we are presenting, and then we come under judgment ourselves. I followed the same procedure for myself that I was instructed to do for Stacie, which was to repent and ask the Lord to forgive my sins and to remove any veil that was over my eyes.

I quickly prayed a prayer of repentance. In my mind, I saw myself in a courtroom, standing before a large bench with a Judge sitting behind it. I said, "Lord, if there is any sin in my life, I repent and ask Your forgiveness. I ask that You would move me from the Courtroom of Judgment to the Throne Room of Grace and Mercy, and remove any veils that have been over the eyes of my understanding so I might see Your truth in every area of my life. Thank You for setting me free and showing me Your truth. Amen."

As soon as I finished my prayer, the Lord removed a veil that had been over my eyes. He spoke and said, "You have cursed the fruit of your womb!" I was shocked. I asked, "How did I do that"? The Holy Spirit brought to my remembrance words that my husband and I had spoken about her during the years of her backslidden condition.

I then repented for the words I had spoken and asked forgiveness. I was also able to stand in the gap on behalf of my husband. Some of the words that we had spoken against her were, "She is being so ignorant!" "She doesn't even see that she is in sin." "It is like she is totally blind to what is happening to her." "The enemy has her." "She won't listen to anything we are saying."

As the words we had spoken about her resounded in my mind, I realized the power of the tongue and how what it says can be used to affect a person. I was truly repentant when I suddenly understood that my daughter had been held as a captive far longer than she needed to, because of the curses we had spoken over her.

While repenting for our own sins of cursing our children by our words, we should repent for any times we haven't honored our parents as we were growing up, and especially during times of adolescent rebellion.

We may have forgotten words we spoke about our parents, but the accuser has a record of them to present to the court. While repenting for ourselves, we should also stand in the gap for our children and any negative things they have said about us.

Children, obey your parents in the Lord, for this is right. "Honor your father and mother," which is the first commandment with promise: "that it may be well with you and you may live long on the earth." And you, fathers, do not provoke your children to wrath, but bring them up in the training and admonition of the Lord. —Ephesians 6:1-4.

As children grow up and become adults, they have many opportunities to be offended by their parents for some reason or another. There is a very good possibility that they spoke against their parents to their friends or others, and judged them harshly. Every parent should take their children into the Courtroom and repent on behalf of possible sins they have committed in the past, or are now committing against you. Forgive them and ask God to forgive them. They could be suffering consequences in their lives because of judging their parents.

This could be a technicality that satan can use against them. I have heard of so many cases where children are not speaking to their parents and have broken off communication with them. These children could be suffering under a curse because of their own words.

Stand in the gap and repent on behalf of the word curses your child may have spoken over you, ask forgiveness and ask the Lord to remove any legal right the enemy has over them in this area.

Another area that the Lord has brought to my attention as we are praying over our generations is the subject of broken vows.

There are 10 vows in particular that are very important to the Lord – the Righteous Judge, and to the accuser. They are the 10 commandments. We should repent and ask forgiveness for the times we, or someone in our lineage, has broken the commandments. Next, decree the positive of each one. An example would be; "Everyone in our generational bloodline will honor their father and mother"

As I finished my prayer, I saw myself standing once again in front of a bench in a Courtroom, with a Judge sitting behind it. His hand was extended to me. I had a manila file in my hand that I saw had the name 'Stacie Strauss' on it. As I looked up at Him, I could literally feel His love for me pouring out of His eyes. I handed the file up to Him. As His hand touched the file, instantly the scripture, which says we will become the head and not the tail, came to life within me. I suddenly realized that satan, using fear, had been wagging me around like the tail of a dog. I knew within myself if satan tried his tricks on me again concerning my daughter, I would always see the picture in my mind of me handing her to the Father God. I knew the Lord loved her much more than her dad or I could.

The next thing that happened was His eyes spoke spirit to spirit to me and said;" I have been waiting for this day when you would truly give Stacie to me."

I thought that I had given her to the father in prayer many times, but now I realized that I would put her on the altar, and then jerk her back off every time I worried about her.

I continued, "I am here to stand in the gap for my daughter, Stacie. I repent on behalf of any sin that she is committing against

You. I ask Your forgiveness on behalf of the sin she is committing against you."

I continued, "I ask that she be moved from the Courtroom of Judgment to the Throne Room of Grace and Mercy for a season of grace in her life. I ask You to remove the veil from the eyes of her understanding so that she will see and embrace Your truth. I ask You to extend this season of grace for as long as it takes for her to see the truth and embrace it."

Then I thanked the Lord for the dream and for how He was going to move on her behalf. I asked if I could be excused; He smiled and nodded. I looked at the clock – it was 4:30 a.m. I immediately got out of bed and went out into the living room and opened my Bible and read from Isaiah.

Shall the prey be taken from the mighty, or the captives of the righteous be delivered? But thus says the Lord: "Even the captives of the mighty shall be taken away, And the prey of the terrible be delivered; for I will contend with him who contends with you, And I will save your children. —Isaiah 49:24-25

You can imagine my excitement as I read this very personal scripture that had come as a direct answer to our cry to the Lord. It had never occurred to us to see her from God's viewpoint—as a "lawful captive".

The other thing that happened when I read the scripture was that the words; "*I will save your children*" jumped out at me. I realized that I had been trying to save her. I don't mean she wasn't saved, but I kept trying to bring her back to the Lord.

The dream, and the results we experienced from following the instructions given by the Lord, have changed the way I pray about every situation. Now as I pray and take each prayer request into the

Courtroom of Heaven, I have a visual of my prayer going before the throne of God, and my faith is increased. I hope my experience will help increase your faith also, so that you can believe that God wants to settle the open cases in your life and give you resolution and victory.

The choice is theirs

As I prayed on behalf of my daughter, I was reminded that we are encouraged in the Bible to pray for others, as Daniel did when he repented on behalf of the sin his entire nation was committing against God. God honored his prayer and supplication.

We, too, are instructed to intercede on behalf of sin that has been committed in our land. God says in 2 Chronicles 7:14, that if we will stand in the gap on behalf of our land, He will heal our nation.

As intercessors, we stand in the gap for individuals, as well as for our nation. I am not saying that by intercession we can save a person. That person still has a responsibility to repent and ask forgiveness for his or her own sin. As intercessors, we are the voice of Jesus on the earth. The Holy Spirit works through us to move them into a position to receive mercy and grace.

By standing in the gap on behalf of sin committed against the Lord by others, we can ask forgiveness and get them moved into grace and mercy for a season, and God is only too happy to remove the veil that satan has been able to cast over them.

Jesus will respond to our plea on their behalf and remove the veil from the eyes of their understanding, give them ears to hear what His Spirit is saying, and a heart to understand. This will give them an opportunity to see the light and the truth and make a choice whether or not they will turn, repent and ask forgiveness for their sins.

Chapter Four

Dream Come True

I began writing down the dream and the scriptures I came across concerning the promises of God for our children. It was early in the morning, still dark. I saw headlights shine through the living room window as someone pulled into our driveway. I went to the door and saw Stacie coming up the steps.

I was surprised to see her. She said she had to run some early morning errands and decided to drive by, saw the lights on and decided to stop. She said, "You are up early, mom, what's up?"

I told her I had a dream about her that woke me up. I asked if she would like to hear it and she said she would. I shared the dream with her and read the confirming scriptures that I had found. She listened intently.

As I finished, I told her I was excited about what the Lord was about to do for her; that He was going to perform a miracle in her life. I felt certain that He would move on her heart and remove a veil from the eyes of her understanding so she would see His truth in areas in her life that she hadn't seen before. I thought that as I was sharing all of this with her, the Lord would immediately remove the veil, but He didn't. Instead, she acted as if nothing out of the ordinary had happened. She thanked me for sharing the dream with her and said she had to get going. She gave me a hug and out the door she went.

Every night, we prayed with new expectation. We went into the Courtroom of Heaven with an Appeal. We decreed the Isaiah 49 scriptures for Stacie, along with some others I had found. Our faith level was so high; we just knew that the Lord was going to move on her life soon. We were close to victory and we knew it!

One week later, the front door burst open; it was Stacie. Before I could say hello she said, "The Lord did it, mom". "He took that veil thing, or whatever it was you told me about, off my eyes, or whatever it was over. I see the truth! I am leaving my old life behind. I can see it is going nowhere. I want to come back home. Let's clean out the spare bedroom."

She moved home that day. About a week after moving home, she asked me if I would go over to her old house with her so she could get her stereo system. I said I would. I didn't let on, but I admit I was a little concerned. We pulled into her old driveway. She sat there a minute, and then said, "I am sick to my stomach. I don't need anything in there. Let's go." So we left, and that was all there was to that old life.

The Lord began to move in her life. I had the dream in 2007. She is now happily married to a man who was raised with the same Christian values. They have two sons and all are doing well. She is still in revival mode with her relationship with the Lord.

Chapter Five

Dream Interpretation

In the dream, the door that I had opened to see into the room was most likely the door of Stacie's heart. The spirit who stepped through the window was the strongman who was guarding his area in her life. The bed represented a stronghold of sin.

The scriptures use the word strongman several times to describe how our enemy binds his captive. The strongman's armor is deception and lies; it's what he trusts in. Because of his pride, he is sure he won't be discovered. He studies his prey and begins his work of enticement and deception.

The strongman in the dream had a legitimate, lawful case against our daughter and he knew it. He trusted that his prey was safe because the charge against her found its strength in her sin. He was using the testimony of her sin in the Courtroom as his spiritual authority to lawfully bind our hands.

The sting of death is sin; and the strength of sin is the law.
—1 Corinthians 15:56

I saw that this particular demonic spirit was surprised to see me in his domain, but he didn't waste any time getting to me. He desired to kill me by choking me, but was prevented from doing me harm. He could only bind my hands, which was a picture of how I felt about the situation—but that was about to change.

I now had knowledge of the offensive tool of the Courtroom. As I used this tool according to the Lord's direction, the law was on my side. I was learning how to legislate from the heavenlies.

Lawful captive of the strongman

When a Christian has knowledge of sin in their life, any sin, and continues in willful disobedience, they are in rebellion against God. While acting in agreement to this sinful way of life they open a door to the enemy, and this makes them a willing or a lawful captive. By their own actions they give the enemy a legal right to rule them.

Whoever commits sin also commits lawlessness, and sin is lawlessness. —1 John 3:4

A 'lawful captive' is a person who is a prisoner legally. They have broken the law, been taken to court and prosecuted, declared guilty, and have found themselves in captivity. The Lord says He will contend for this lawful captive. The Lord will use His intercessors to stand in the gap for the sin the person has committed to get the legal rights of the enemy removed and the captive delivered.

Some think that an intercessor has to be a person who is in their closet praying all the time. This is not true. There is the office of intercessor, but not everyone has this calling. However, praying for someone other than yourself is intercession.

The deception often comes in an area of weakness where the person is easily tempted. Eventually they are in complete deception, sometimes actually believing that, in some way, the Lord excuses what they are doing. They usually won't listen to a concerned friend or family member about the danger they are in, but in love, we must still try to bring truth to them. It is important to note that if we try to convince anyone of their sin and they don't listen, we must not be offended or resentful towards them and begin to judge them. In so doing we become a lawful captive ourselves.

Tricks of the enemy

This reminds me of an example of how the enemy deceives a person until they let their guard down and a veil of deception comes over them. When they least expect it, the enemy can throw his net over them. This story is about an animal, but the principal is the same.

When our children were teenagers, they asked for a snake as a pet. One of their friends had one they didn't want anymore. I don't like snakes but we decided to let them have it for a little while. We thought that they might get used to snakes and not be afraid of them.

This snake, like all snakes, ate mice. I would watch as they put a mouse in the cage with the snake. At first, the mouse would be a nervous wreck. He would stay in the far corner, eyeing the snake. He would shake and shiver. Soon, when the snake didn't move, he would get braver and move around in the pen. After about an hour, if the snake still hadn't moved, he would be brave enough to even run around it and climb up on it. He got so used to the snake that within a short period of time, maybe an hour and a half, he would actually be sitting right in front of the snake's mouth with his back to the snake. He would be cleaning himself, totally unaware of the danger he was in. Suddenly the snake would strike and the mouse was trapped in his crushing grip.

The snake provided me with a powerful visual spiritual object lesson to share with our children and their friends. I would talk to them about the dangers of taking their enemy, the devil, for granted. After all, he is a snake and we are his prey.

At a basic level, that snake knew he was going to eat this mouse, but he waited until the mouse forgot to be on alert. The mouse didn't realize the dangerous position he was in. If the snake was able to reason, he would have been secure in the knowledge the mouse was his and he didn't have to worry about it getting away. It was in his domain. If I had decided to become an intercessor for that mouse and take him out of the pen, the snake wouldn't have been able to accomplish his goal

Bind the strong man and rescue his prey

Assuredly, I say to you, whatever you bind on earth will be bound in heaven, and whatever you loose on earth will be loosed in heaven. —Mathew 18:18

When a strong man, fully armed, guards his own palace, his goods are in peace. But when a stronger than he comes upon him and overcomes him, he takes from him all his armor in which he trusted, and divides his spoils. —Luke 11:21-22

When we find out the truth and apply it on behalf of his victim, we become the stronger one by using our legal rights in their correct order: repentance, forgiveness, applying the blood of Jesus, and then legally removing his captive from him. When the Holy Spirit prompts you to intercede for another, do not take it lightly. We may be the only person praying for them.

Or how can one enter a strong man's house and plunder his goods, unless he first binds the strong man? And then he will plunder his house. —Matthew 12:29 KJV

I had thought the way to bind the enemy was just to say," I bind you in the name of Jesus." I have done this many times over the years, but now I wonder how effective that was. It didn't occur to me to remove his legal rights before I said, "I bind you." In reality, according to the Word, I didn't have the authority to bind him if sin was involved. Psalm 149:5-9 explains how to bind the enemy. The word bind means to constrain with legal authority.

Let the saints be joyful in glory; Let them sing aloud on their beds. Let the high praises of God be in their mouth, And a two-edged sword in their hand, To execute vengeance on the nations, And punishments on the peoples; To bind their kings with chains, And their nobles with fetters of iron; To execute on them the written judgment—This honor have all His saints. Praise the LORD! —Psalm 149:5-9.

This scripture says that as the saints sing aloud on their beds, the powers over nations and people are bound. It doesn't say anything about requiring human strength. It doesn't say why the saint is in bed. This is particularly exciting to the saint who is in the bed for health or age related reasons. They may think that they aren't as valuable as one who can go out to the meetings and pray.

According to this scripture, the Lord is saying that the saints on their beds can execute the judgment written against these principalities and powers. Their power and strength in intercession is the Word and their joyful song.

One night while meditating on this scripture, I asked the Lord, "What is the difference between praise and high praise? If high praise is what binds the spiritual kings or principalities and powers with chains and the nobles with fetters of iron, is 'high praise' when we move into a higher spiritual level during praise and worship?" I was thinking about the transition from lively clapping during praise into slow, more worshipful songs.

I woke up later that night hearing these words spoken loudly in my spirit: "High praise is not an emotion." There was a pause, then the voice continued, "Highest praise is My Word being quoted back to Me. My Word is the highest praise to My ears." High praise is the Word of God!

The scripture in Psalm 149 also mentions the sword in our hand, which we know is the Word. It will bind the enemy as we use it by quoting or singing it. Once he is bound, then we can rescue the prey that he has captured; we can plunder his camp.

Praise as lawgiver

One word for praise is Judah, and a definition for the word Judah is lawgiver.

And she conceived again and bore a son, and said, "Now I will praise the LORD." Therefore she called his name Judah. —Genesis 29:35

The next scripture reveals that praise (Judah) is a lawgiver.

Gilead is mine: Manasseh is mine; Ephraim also is the strength of mine head; Judah is my lawgiver.—Psalm 108:8 KJV

We see that high praise (the Word) and the law cannot be separated. During times of worship, as we sing songs of praise that are composed of scripture, we are creating an altar to the Lord and establishing truth on the earth. This is called 'worshipping in spirit and truth.'

But the hour is coming, and now is, when the true worshipers will worship the Father in spirit and truth; for the Father is seeking such to worship Him. God is Spirit, and those who worship Him must worship in spirit and truth. —John 4:23

Sanctify them by Your truth. Your word is truth.— John 17:1

As we read the Word aloud, it gives the Word a voice that is spoken of in scripture. The angels listen for and respond to this voice. We can quote the Word by speaking it or by singing, and the enemy will be bound by the Word of God. God Himself is bound by His Word.

Our enemy will be defeated by our skillful use of the sword (the Word of God) that we wield against him. Because praise is associated with lawgiver, it is done legally in the Courtroom of Heaven.

Bless the LORD, you His angels, Who excel in strength, who do His word, Heeding the voice of His word. —Psalm 103:20

Picture the angels crowding into your room to listen to the Word. As you read and decree particular scriptures that contain directives, the angels will be sent to fight the battle that is going on over your situation.

Commission given to believers

It seems that even though the commission to believers is to execute the judgment against the enemy while we are on the earth, things have been turned around and the enemy is using the authority of the Word of God to get judgment executed against us.

He can bring accusations against us because of our words, with our sin used as evidence in the Courtroom of Heaven. We may not be aware of where the attack is coming from, and won't seem to be able to get relief from our problems.

This could cause some to lose faith and move into unbelief, which is the enemy's plan. The truth has been hidden from us because of our sin. We aren't able to exercise our authority and achieve dominion over him unless we are in right standing before the Lord

The enemy travels to and fro on the earth finding victims. The accuser wasn't cast into hell when he was thrown down from heaven, but cast onto the earth to be punished by the Church. We aren't able to exercise our authority and achieve dominion over him unless we are in right standing before the Lord. He is just doing his job. He will continue doing this accusing and getting judgments against believers, until Jesus returns and puts him in chains for his everlasting punishment.

Seize your opportunity

Show up where you aren't expected, where your adversary the accuser, also known as satan, is playing the part of the Prosecuting Attorney presenting his case.

As believers, our purpose in the Courtroom of Heaven is to make intercession as an Ambassador of Reconciliation, to stand in the gap on behalf of humans, regions, governments, nations, or any other case the Lord leads.

Chapter Six

The Judge

Order in the Court – on earth as it is in heaven

The Word mentions that there are the same officials present in the Courtroom of Heaven that would be participants in a case being tried on earth. The highest official in either courtroom is the judge.

The participants in the heavenly Courtroom are:

- The Righteous Judge, who is the Lord.

…. and the heavens shall declare his righteousness: for God is judge himself. —Psalm 50:6

- A prosecuting attorney, known as the accuser of the brethren—also known as satan or lucifer.
- The Defendant, who is the victim or the prey.
- The Ambassador of Reconciliation, also known as the intercessor believer.
- The Advocate, who is Jesus Christ the Living Word.

He is coming to judge the earth. With righteousness He shall judge the world, and the peoples with equity. —Psalm 98:9

The Word is what judges the believer in this life. When we accept Christ as our personal Savior, we are taking a vow to obey

Him. To obey Him is to obey His Word. If we disobey His Word we are in rebellion, and our rebellion is what will capture us and take us into this Courtroom in heaven.

In scripture, Jesus Christ is referred to as the Living Word.

In the beginning was the Word, and the Word was with God, and the Word was God. —John 1:1

And the Word was made flesh, and dwelt among us, and we beheld his glory, the glory as of the only begotten of the Father, full of grace and truth —John 1:14

Every Scripture is God-breathed (given by His inspiration) and profitable for instruction, for reproof and conviction of sin, for correction of error and discipline in obedience, [and] for training in righteousness (in holy living, in conformity to God's will in thought, purpose, and action), So that the man of God may be complete and proficient, well fitted and thoroughly equipped for every good work. —2 Timothy 3:16-17 AMP

This heavenly Courtroom can be compared to a courtroom on the earth. When cases are brought before a judge on earth, specific laws and conditions determine the direction they take. It is the same in the Courtroom of Heaven. The Lord is compelled by the law of His Word to uphold His divine judicial order, even if He is grieved and wants to pardon His children so they don't have to suffer. He has to remain impartial; He won't violate His own laws.

The Lord has to render judgment on the one in sin. This could be any type of sin. The Lord is on our side, but He has to listen to the enemy present evidence against us in the Courtroom of Heaven. This has to be very difficult for Him to have to sit and listen to the enemy accuse us.

Contrary to some opinions, the Lord is not some cruel, spiteful God waiting for His creation to do something wrong so He can smite them. To prove His love He sent Jesus, who loved all mankind enough to lay down His life for us on the cross. He wants all to be saved.

A judge on the earth takes an oath to uphold the law of the land and to judge fairly to the best of his ability. Even so, there is opportunity for corruption and injustice, unlike in the Courtroom of Heaven where the truth will prevail. In the courtroom on earth when we come before the judge, we make a vow to tell the whole truth and nothing but the truth. We even say, "So help me God." Man can decide not to pay attention to the vow and lie, and may get away with it, but not in the Courtroom of Heaven.

Righteousness and Justice are the foundation of your throne. Mercy and truth go before your face. —Psalm 89:14

The Judge may even be called to testify against us.

He judges and pronounces the sentence.

Against You, You only, have I sinned and done that which is evil in Your sight, So that You are justified when You speak [Your sentence] and faultless in Your judgment. —Psalm 51:4 AMP

The Israelites understood how the Court in heaven operated

We see an example of Israel repenting for their sin against God because they realized they were being judged because of their sin, and it had made them lawful captives of the enemy. They realized that their sins and those of their ancestors were testifying against them. They realized that the country was cursed, and because of it they were going through a drought that was divine judgment.

Oh Lord, though our iniquities testify against us, do it (forgive) for your names sake, for our backslidings are many. We have sinned against You. —Jeremiah 14:7

In verse 20, they go on to pray about generational sins that had also contributed their part in the judgment and opened the door for a curse to come upon their bloodlines. They said,

"We acknowledge, Oh Lord, our wickedness and the iniquity of our fathers." (verse 20)

You can appeal injustices in the Courtroom

If you have had a case in an earthly court and there was a sentence imposed or a judgment that was an injustice, the Lord has a solution to give you hope. The Lord was present and heard every testimony. He is faithful and just and He will recompense. It is never too late to appeal an injustice to the highest court, the Court of Heaven.

There are cases of injustice where the person hasn't done anything wrong. The enemy has attacked and plundered, and the person can't figure out why this has happened to him or her. We see an example of this in the book of Job, a man who was righteous before the Lord. In Job 1:1-7 and Job 2:1-7, the Lord gave satan permission to touch Job and all that he had. This was a test, not only for Job but also for his friends. In spite of not being able to understand why all this happened to him, Job stood firm in his faith in God, but Job's wife was angry at God.

Are you mad at God?

Recently someone told me while they were praying for God to heal them, that God revealed to them that they were angry at Him for something that had happened earlier. He didn't solve a previous problem in their life the way they expected Him to. That unmet expectation caused them to be mad at God and they weren't aware of it. It had allowed a root of bitterness to take hold. They went on to share that they repented and received forgiveness. They then commanded the root of bitterness to go and they asked the Lord to fill the empty place with His love. In a short period of time, their health issues resolved themselves.

Some of us have had an opportunity to get angry at God. We could have hidden anger against God and not even know it. When we do that, we don't realize it's a form of judgment against Him. Over time, this anger could cause a bitter root to develop that needs to be addressed by repenting and asking for forgiveness in prayer. This bitter root blocks communications between God and us, and could even be the cause of unresolved health issues.

Back to Job

The scripture says, in Job 42:6, that Job repented and the Lord blessed him with twice as much as he had lost. If you feel that you are a victim of injustice, pray and take your case into the Courtroom of Heaven. Ask the Judge for justice in the form of compensation of wrong done to you. Seek the Holy Spirit for what to ask for as compensation; He will be faithful to speak to you. Ask for repayment of all that has been stolen. The Lord wants to settle your case and render justice on your behalf.

Compensation cases on earth are expensive, but not in heaven. On earth, some believers aren't able to afford the cost to appeal their case to a higher court, so they feel hopeless. As believers, we can go boldly into Court knowing the price has been paid in full. Once you take the case into that highest court, the real Supreme Court, you will feel a huge burden lift off you and can be assured the law of God will begin to work on behalf of your petition. Don't let the enemy rob you of your peace over what is happening or what might appear to be out of control.

God's time is not our time. While we wait, we can be comforted knowing that He is working on our behalf. The Lord is faithful to keep us and our loved ones safe during trials. He says that as we go through these trials, we will be refined and come forth as gold.

> *But He knows the way that I take [He has concern for it, appreciates, and pays attention to it]. When He has tried me, I shall come forth as refined gold [pure and luminous].*
> *—Job 23:10 AMP*

I have had people ask me how they would know which heavenly court to plead their case in. I don't have the answer to that question. It seems that whichever court in heaven a person would appear in, they would stand before the same Judge.

I encourage them not to let confusion in this area stop them from going into the Courtroom of Heaven. I just always preface my prayer with the words; "I am coming into your Courtroom in Heaven." It has worked for me for the past 10 years so I am sure it will work for you too.

Testimony

Not too long ago, I was a member of a prayer group that felt led of the Holy Spirit to take a government official into the Courtroom of Heaven. This person was known to be sympathetic to the Communist agenda. We knew this because the news had been covering this official's visits as an ambassador representing the United States to Communist countries, and had been reporting that this person was saying things that didn't necessarily reflect America's position correctly.

While in prayer, we asked the Lord for a strategy to pray for the truth to be exposed in this person's life. We felt the Lord told us to petition Him under the "Freedom of Information Act". Although we had never heard of this before, we did as He instructed. Within a week this person's true beliefs were exposed in ways that only God could orchestrate.

It was amazing the way the truth of the person's beliefs was exposed. During an interview on a national news channel, the person was asked to name the two most important people they admired and had made the biggest contribution in forming their life standards, someone that they might call their mentor. In their pride, this person boldly proclaimed the names of two Communist leaders. Wow, was there a ruckus! Because the truth had been broadcast on national television, the official was fired from their high government position. We weren't praying for anything like that, and we didn't have any preconceived ideas as to what the Lord was going to do, but he answered the petition we had made in His Courtroom. I am sure that the Lord put the words in the reporter's mouth to ask the right questions, whether he was aware of it or not.

Since that time, we have used this strategy in other cases with amazing results. The results didn't always come in a week, but we consistently had results within a year. We don't do this in judgment. Sometimes good things can come to light, and with it are public rewards.

The Judge loves to reward His people.

It might seem that the Judge only renders judgment for sin, but this is not true. He also loves to see His children in the Courtroom so he can reward them for righteousness.

In 2 Chronicles 2, Solomon asked not only for judgment on his enemies, but to be justified (rewarded).

Then hear thou in heaven, and do, and judge thy servants, condemning the wicked, to bring his way upon his head; and justifying the righteous, to give him according to his righteousness. —2 Chronicles 6:23 KJV

Sometimes the Word judgment brings fear, but it doesn't need to. Judgment means to make a decision. Some decisions we like and some we don't.

Testimony of Judgment for Righteousness

My name is Mark Williamson. My dad is Frank Williamson, a pastor in Ft. Walton Beach, Florida. I had a dream about him that I would like to share.

My dad is a quiet, humble sort of guy who goes about doing good but not letting people know where he and my mom sow their seed unto the Lord. In the dream, I was surprised to see my dad and me in a courtroom. I sat there watching. I saw the Judge standing behind the bench and my dad was standing in front of him. The Judge was huge, very tall, and my dad looked very small in comparison. The Judge had a scroll in His hands, and as this scroll began to unroll, it went down to the floor. The Judge was reading it to Himself as it was unrolling. When it finished unrolling and He was finished reading, He looked at my father and said; "Frank Williamson, after reading your testimony, I find you guilty as charged". I thought to myself, "Oh no. What has my dad done?" The Judge read the charges that were on the scroll.

He said; "Frank Williamson, I find you guilty of feeding, leading and protecting My flock."

"I find you guilty of having compassion on the poor and the widows."

"I find you guilty of seeking My will and being obedient to My will even in the face of adversity."

"I find you guilty of being faithful. I find you guilty of loving the unlovely, and even at times in your life when you have been betrayed; you have forgiven and loved others as I do."

He went on to read some more wonderful guilty verdicts over my dad. There were things that had been recorded about my dad during his whole lifetime. I don't remember them all. Then the Lord said, "For your judgment, I am rewarding you by giving you a treasure of My heart -- Times of Refreshing." Then the gavel came down. I know now that when the gavel falls in heaven, there is a reaction on the earth.

"Times of Refreshing" is an actual place. The Lord had given my parents a vision for a Christian retreat center. He brought this mansion to their attention because it was on land that backed up to their land. It had been a Christian-based healing ministry mansion throughout the 1980's and was now in the court system. When it was brought to the attention of my parents, they prayed for the Lord's will and for provision, if this property was His plan for them.

It is a long miraculous story, but the end result is that my dad was awarded this mansion by a judge in a courtroom setting on earth. This dream revealed how it was awarded in heaven before it was awarded on earth. Now my parents are holding Christian retreats there on a regular basis. The prophetic word has been fulfilled.

Times of Refreshing Christian Retreat

Earthly inheritance

There are inheritances that the Lord wants to bless us with on this earth, as well as spiritual inheritances that He has planned for us from the beginning of time.

> *Take heed that you do not do your charitable deeds before men, to be seen by them. Otherwise you have no reward from your Father in heaven. Therefore, when you do a charitable deed, do not sound a trumpet before you as the hypocrites do in the synagogues and in the streets, that they may have glory from men. Assuredly, I say to you, they have their reward. But when you do a charitable deed, do not let your left hand know what your right hand is doing, that your charitable deed may be in secret; and your Father who sees in secret will Himself reward you openly.*
> *—Matthew 6:1-4*

You may want to seek the Lord about any inheritance that has been stolen from you in this life. You may or may not be aware of an injustice if it was something that happened in a past generation. Some have lost financial inheritances through injustices and, in some cases, it may appear as if there is no hope of it being restored. This could effectively block a person from moving beyond the unfairness of the situation and make it difficult to fully inherit God's peace.

As you bring your case into the Courtroom of Heaven, the thief will have to appear in answer to a summons from the Judge. As you address the Judge, explain that you are there to petition Him for a resolution in the case of an inheritance due you and your family.

Here is a sample prayer regarding an earthly inheritance:

Your Honor, I am here before You to present a petition to have any inheritance restored that has been stolen from me or my family. (You can name it specifically if you know what it is.)

I am standing in the gap for myself and my generational bloodline from its earliest beginnings. I repent on behalf of any sin that may have been committed against You by any of my ancestors, myself or any other family member. I renounce all witchcraft and occult associations. I ask that you would forgive our sins as we forgive those who have sinned against us. Please wash our family bloodline with the blood of Jesus, cleansing, purifying and redeeming us, that your plans and purposes for our lives would be accomplished. As you cleanse my generational bloodline from sin, I thank You for removing all legal rights any curses may have had to operate within my bloodline. I now command any demons that were attached or assigned to the curses to see they come to fruition in each generation, to go—you are fired—you no longer have a job. I ask You, Your Honor, to replace the curses with blessings upon our family.

I thank You that, as I have repented, Your Word says You are faithful to forgive. I thank You for moving my family into the Throne Room of Grace and Mercy, where we will be able to freely receive all that has been stolen from us and all that You have stored up for us.

I thank You that Your Word says in Proverbs 6:31, when the thief is caught he will have to restore seven-fold what he has stolen. You say in Psalm 47:4 that You will choose our inheritance. I confess and accept that my reward may not be in the form that I am looking for, but it will be restored to me in the way that You choose to bless me.

Thank you, Your Honor, for hearing my case and executing justice on my behalf. Amen.

Spiritual inheritance

It is possible that someone reading this has a spiritual inheritance they have turned their back on. This could include a number of different things. As you ask the Lord, He will be faithful to reveal if there is unfinished business between you and Him that needs to be addressed. An example of a lost spiritual inheritance could involve a person who has been called to be an evangelist or a missionary but didn't follow through, even though they knew of the call on their life. It isn't too late; the Lord is waiting.

Here is a sample prayer regarding a spiritual inheritance. You can change the wording to fit your particular situation.

Your Honor, I come into Your Courtroom today to thank You for placing a call on my life before I was in my mother's womb. You said of me: "Before I formed you in the womb I knew you; before you were born I sanctified you; I ordained you a prophet to the nations." (Jeremiah 1:5)

You have called me to go to the nations and to evangelize the lost. I repent for the fact that I have not accomplished what You ordained me to do. I ask forgiveness for this sin because I know the enemy has been able to hinder my spiritual and physical walk because of my rebellion to the call on my life. I ask that you would move me from the Courtroom of Judgment into the Throne Room of Grace and Mercy, and show me what I am to do next to fulfill all that You have ordained for me.

I ask that as I have cleared up the spiritual legal issues in this case, and you have forgiven me, that the enemy would no longer be able to punish me for my rebellion. I ask that you would heal any infirmities or any mental, physical, or financial attacks that have been able to steal from me in the past because of this unsettled matter.

I thank You that Your Word says that if I am willing, You will lead me into my spiritual inheritance. I am willing. Amen.

As you receive your earthly or spiritual inheritances, or if you have already received an inheritance, ask the Lord if you are spending it correctly, or if there is something He wants you to do with what He has given you. You may be surprised at His answer!

*And I heard a loud voice
saying in heaven,
now is come salvation, and
strength, and the kingdom
of our God, and the power
of his Christ: for the
accuser of our brethren is
cast down, which accused
them before our God
day and night.*
Revelation 12:10

Chapter Seven

The Prosecutor

His tricks and our options

The prosecutor is also known as the accuser of the brethren, also satan, or Lucifer.

And I heard a loud voice saying in heaven, now is come salvation, and strength, and the kingdom of our God, and the power of his Christ: for the accuser of our brethren is cast down, which accused them before our God day and night. —Revelation 12:10

The accuser is obviously in some type of courtroom setting when he is doing this accusing. I used to think this was at the White Throne of Judgment, but that isn't true; he doesn't wait around for that setting. I don't believe for a minute that he could stand to be in the presence of the Lord, where the angels and saints are worshipping in the Throne Room, but he is in one of the courts in heaven.

This scripture seems to point to a courtroom setting.

I saw the Lord sitting on His throne, and all the host of heaven standing by, on His right hand and on His left. And the Lord said, 'Who will persuade Ahab to go up, that he may fall at Ramoth Gilead?' So one spoke in this manner, and another spoke in that manner. Then a spirit came forward and stood before the Lord, and said, 'I will persuade him.' The Lord said to him, 'In what way?' So he said, 'I will go out and be a lying spirit in the mouth of all his prophets.' And the Lord said, "You shall persuade him, and also prevail. Go out and do so." — I Kings 22:19-22.

Accuser: complainant at law; specifically, satan. The word devil comes from the Greek word *diabolos*, which means "accuser". In early Judaism, satan was recognized as a prosecutor in God's court, with God being the ultimate Judge. In the original Hebrew, satan is not a proper name, but a title. The Hebrew term ha-satan or "the satan," can be translated as "the prosecutor."

(http://criminaldefenselawyertx.com/satan-was-a-prosecutor-jesus-was-a-defense-lawyer)

This spiritual prosecutor is accusing the saints before God day and night. It is logical to assume that he must stand to gain something in the life of the believer or he wouldn't waste his time. He has to take advantage of every fleeting moment that he has while the believer is still living on this earth. His goal is to make our lives as miserable as possible, and maybe draw us away from the Lord and into his slave camp.

Every Christian's life will be examined at some time in this Courtroom. This Courtroom can also be the place to run for refuge and protection. When there is an injustice coming against us, we have an opportunity to change the situation through intercessory prayer.

Every Christian is responsible to abide by the law of the Word, just as we abide by the law of the land on earth. On earth, our goal is to live within the law and stay out of the courtroom. Just as problems on earth are often resolved in a courtroom, so spiritual problems are resolved in the Courtroom of Heaven.

Scripture shows us that satan can stand in the presence of God. Some might ask," How can satan not be in the Throne Room and yet stand in the presence of God? Scripture talks of him "presenting himself before the Lord."

Now there was a day when the sons of God came to present themselves before the Lord, and Satan also came among them. And the Lord said to Satan, "From where do you come?" So Satan answered the Lord and said, "From going to and fro on the earth, and from walking back and forth on it." —Job 1:6-7

Again there was a day when the sons of God came to present themselves before the Lord, and satan came also among them to present himself before the Lord. —Job 2:1

Then he showed me Joshua the high priest standing before the Angel of the Lord, and satan standing at his right hand to oppose him. —Zechariah 3:1

A scripture in Zechariah speaks of courts and judgment.

*Thus says the Lord of Hosts; 'If you will walk in My ways, and if you will keep My command, Then you shall also judge My house, and likewise have charge of My courts; I will give you places to walk among these who stand here.
—Zechariah 3:7*

Tactics of the enemy

If we are aware of the resources he uses to deceive us, we will be alert to his wiles and be on guard. We can be tempted by something that seems innocent, but it can lead us down a wrong path. This allows the accuser to obtain a guilty verdict over our lives and lawfully take us captive.

Jesus answered them, Be careful that no one misleads you [deceiving you and leading you into error]. —Matthew 24:4 AMP

The Word says the enemy was created to be the anointed covering cherub.

> *You were the anointed cherub who covers; I established you; You were on the holy mountain of God; You walked back and forth in the midst of fiery stones.* —Ezekiel 28:14

He was given a powerful anointing by God and his title was the 'anointed covering cherub.' It is possible he retained the anointing when he was cast out of heaven. The Bible says the Lord's gifts and callings are irrevocable, and that He is no respecter of persons.

> *For the gifts and the calling of God are irrevocable.*
> —Romans 11:29

The enemy has taken it upon himself to use his anointing to cover the eyes of the understanding of mankind through deception. This "cover" or veil can blind us to the fact that we are in a battle with a real enemy for our eternal lives. Most of us are so busy with life and its difficulties that we don't think about turning the tables on him, or even think about the source or root of our problems.

> *In fact, their minds were grown hard and calloused [they had become dull and had lost the power of understanding]; for until this present day, when the Old Testament is being read, that same veil still lies [on their hearts], not being lifted [to reveal] that in Christ it is made void and done away. Yes, down to this [very] day whenever Moses is read, a veil lies upon their minds and hearts.* —2 Corinthians 3:14-15 AMP

Even though this scripture refers to the Old Testament, it is used in the present tense. It says, "To this very day there is a veil." Verse 16 goes on to say,

> *But whenever a person turns [in repentance] to the Lord, the veil is stripped off and taken away.*

Defeat the prosecuting attorney's strategies

We have to respect the position of the prosecuting attorney, the accuser, who is at times described as a 'principality' or 'power'. The definition of *principality* is the position, territory or legal jurisdiction that is ruled by a prince. No matter how badly we want to direct righteous indignation toward him, we must keep our wits about us. We are there to plead for mercy and grace, and then justice. The only way to obtain justice against him is to do it by the written Word. Our Mentor, Jesus, was able to keep His cool when conversing with satan. The Lord is not ruffled in the least by him. The Word says that the Lord is over every principality and power. They are created for His purposes and they are subject to Him.

For by Him all things were created that are in heaven and that are on earth, visible and invisible, whether thrones or dominions or principalities or powers. All things were created through Him and for Him. —Colossians 1:16

In the desert, when the enemy came to Jesus with temptations, He answered by quoting scripture and saying, "It is written." Scripture seems to imply that Jesus answered in a matter of fact, civil tone. He didn't dispute, rebuke or yell at satan. He wasn't disrespectful. Jesus simply quoted the scripture, and when the enemy was done tempting him, he left. No argument!

Then Jesus was led up by the Spirit into the wilderness to be tempted by the devil. And when He had fasted forty days and forty nights, afterward He was hungry. Now when the tempter came to Him, he said, "If You are the Son of God, command that these stones become bread." But He answered and said, "It is written, 'Man shall not live by bread alone, but by every word that proceeds from the mouth of God.'" Then the devil took Him up into the holy

city, set Him on the pinnacle of the temple, and said to Him, "If You are the Son of God, throw Yourself down. For it is written:' He shall give His angels charge over you,' and,' In their hands they shall bear you up, Lest you dash your foot against a stone.'" Jesus said to him, "It is written again, 'You shall not tempt the LORD your God.'"Again, the devil took Him up on an exceedingly high mountain, and showed Him all the kingdoms of the world and their glory. And he said to Him, "All these things I will give You if You will fall down and worship me." Then Jesus said to him, "Away with you, Satan! For it is written, 'You shall worship the LORD your God, and Him only you shall serve.'" Then the devil left Him, and behold, angels came and ministered to Him.
—Matthew 4:1-11

Courtroom protocol

There is a protocol to be adhered to when we are dealing with the prosecutor in the Courtroom.

As I reflect on my more than 30 years of experience in intercession and spiritual warfare, I know that many times I have used the words, "I bind you satan", and I have said things like, "I come against you, satan," or "I come against the principality of abortion," or any other principality that happened to be our prayer focus. Never once did I think about the fact that he might have a legal right from the Judge to be operating in the situation. It was presumptuous and dangerous for me to pray this way, and scripturally unlawful. I was guilty of attacking principalities and powers, because I was just blindly following what I had observed was the way to conduct spiritual warfare.

As I commanded principalities and powers to be bound and rebuked them, I did not realize that I was actually attacking what

God had put in place. Even though it was demonic, it still has permission of the Judge because of the legal rights it obtains from the Judge in the area of its jurisdiction. Because of my dream, I have learned to keep the "I" out of the warfare. When we say "I", we are saying that as a physical human being, "I" am personally coming against a spiritual entity to fight. This is an invitation to the enemy to attack us personally or to attack someone in our family who may be a weaker link, all because we aren't bringing the Lord into the equation. Satan used the word "I" as he described what he would do (Isaiah 14:11-13), and it was viewed by the Lord as pride.

There is no place in the Bible where a human being said, "I rebuke you satan."

As discussed earlier, since the Lord is over all principalities and powers, satan is subject to the authority of God. In some cases, rebuking satan could be considered rebellion against God's divine order, and could open a door the enemy could use to take God's people captive.

Testimony — saved from deception

By standing in the gap on behalf of sin committed against the Lord by others, we can ask forgiveness, and get them moved into grace and mercy. God is happy to remove the veil from the eyes of their understanding that satan had been able to cast over them. Here is a testimony to God's goodness.

Praise God for His faithfulness. We pastor a church and have been in ministry almost 30 years. As pastors, we saw our daughter go through a divorce after an emotionally abusive marriage. The trauma in her marriage had left her emotionally numb, and opened her up to wrong relationships, leaving her devastated. The enemy tried to destroy her life. From being a protected pastor's daughter, raised in ministry her whole life, leading worship for our church and being involved in our youth ministry, we saw our daughter pull away from her church friends and make friends with the world.

The world tried to swallow her up. Within months she ended up getting raped, doing drugs and alcohol, and started working for and dancing in a nightclub. We needed a miracle for our daughter because we knew the call of God on her life. Just months before all "hell broke loose" in her life, she had received a prophetic word that God was going to use her in the worship ministry and that she would travel the world leading worship for ministries and writing songs. She'd just returned from worship at a 15,000 member church in Africa, and she had been invited to lead worship for a conference with one of Americas leading ministries. Yet, at the very time she should have been on that stage leading worship for that conference, she had been derailed by the plan of the enemy.

During my daughter's difficult season I must add, she loved God with all her heart and would not miss church for anything. She was the first to be at the church every Sunday. She held onto the Lord with everything, no matter where she had been the night before.

We made the decision to love our daughter because we represented the heart of God to her. Our love kept her and her 2-year-old son in our home. People in our church judged us for not kicking her out of our home; those people left our church. Our daughter became our prodigal.

We brought Jeanette to our ministry, thinking she was there just to teach on worshipping with flags and the dance, but the Lord had a higher plan. Jeanette and her husband stayed in our home. One day as we sat on the couch in my living room, she shared with me about the Courtroom of Heaven and offered to pray in agreement with me for my daughter. I had told her we felt it was urgent for our daughter to have her eyes opened, to see that the new friends she had and the places she was involved with were not a safe place. We knew she needed to make a choice to cut herself off from a world that was trying to ensnare her and steal her away from us.

Jeanette and I prayed the prayer according to God's Word, and by faith brought my daughter's case into the Courtroom of Heaven. We declared together that the devil could no longer have her and he had to leave her alone and set her free. I had specifically prayed that my daughter would see that she needed to walk away from the world she was being drawn into.

Within one week of praying together with Jeanette, the devil tried one more time. It was a Sunday night and her job at the nightclub ended at 9:00 p.m. She was running a clothing boutique for the nightclub. Because she had gotten a DUI she wasn't able to drive, so my husband was going to drive to the club to pick her up. She had texted us that she was done early and was waiting for him. She walked to a nearby pub and ordered a coke and was waiting for his call to say he was there.

When my husband got to her work place she was nowhere to be found. She was not answering our text messages or her phone. My husband waited until after midnight and then we called the police, knowing something was wrong.

We knew the enemy was trying one more time to take her out. In the early hours of the morning, she called and shared with us what had happened. She believed that while she was in that pub waiting for us to pick her up, someone had slipped a date rape drug into her coke. There were a group of men flirting with her but she had ignored them. She had no memory of what had happened except that someone had found her on the sidewalk at 2:00 a.m. and knew that she had been drugged. She was shaky and her thoughts were *jumbled. The person who found her took her to a safe place until we could come and pick her up. On our way home she shared, "Mom, I'm not going back to work. I'm not going back to that area. I thought I could handle it, but I'm not going back there. I need to get away. I need to get out of town."*

The Lord had answered our prayer. Within weeks, our daughter was on a plane to a powerful ministry of some friends of ours where she had been hired on staff. She went to Bible school and was able to have a safe place to heal and be restored. Today she is married to a wonderful godly man, is leading worship in our church, and is involved with ministering to children, getting them on fire for God and teaching them about the anointing of God. The anointing on her life is so powerful. She is fearless and bold in winning souls and exposing the plan of the enemy in people's lives. She has a passion for young people who are going through trauma. The devil had to release our daughter. The very week Jeanette and I prayed, all heaven moved on our behalf and my daughter was set free!!!

Deceptions of the enemy

One of the biggest challenges for Christians is in the area of unforgiveness. Some think, "Well I don't think it will matter, and besides I have every excuse to be angry." This isn't about our reasons for being angry. It is straight- forward—forgive others or God can't forgive you. If you don't forgive, you are open to being deceived.

Jesus tells a parable about a man who was forgiven a huge debt, and then turned around and put someone who owed him a very small amount into jail because he couldn't pay. This is what Jesus said would happen to such a person:

And his master was angry and delivered him to the torturers until he should pay all that was due to him. So my Heavenly

Father also will do to you if each of you, from his heart, does not forgive his brother his trespasses. —Matthew 18:34-35

This is the deepening effect of unforgiveness, a warning regarding the danger of tolerated or embraced un-forgiveness. Unforgiveness, like poison, can permeate and bind the soul, ultimately corrupting everything around it. The foremost key to deliverance from entrenched bondage in a believer's life is the act of forgiveness. Forgiving others from our heart flushes out the poison with the power of the cross. Unforgiveness can lead down paths we would have never imagined. *(Commentary)*

Another area of deception

Another tactic of the enemy is to prompt Christians to judge each other. In this scripture, we see a warning to Christians about the consequences of judging each other.

DO NOT judge and criticize and condemn others, so that you may not be judged and criticized and condemned yourselves. For just as you judge and criticize and condemn others, you will be judged and criticized and condemned, and in accordance with the measure you [use to] deal out to others, it will be dealt out again to you. —Matthew 7:1-2 AMP

The Word says that if we judge others the Lord will turn us over to satan, but not because He wants to. The Lord is always thinking about correction or discipline for the purpose of redemption and restoration.

Deliver such as one unto Satan for the destruction of the flesh, that the spirit may be saved in the day of the Lord Jesus. —I Corinthians 5:5

Paul considered judging others a serious enough offense that he warned believers not even to take communion until they have settled all differences.

> *Therefore, whoever eats the bread or drinks the cup of the Lord in an unworthy manner will be guilty of sinning against the body and blood of the Lord. A man ought to examine himself before he eats of the bread and drinks of the cup. For anyone who eats and drinks without recognizing the body of the Lord eats and drinks judgment on himself. That is why many among you are weak and sick and a number of you have fallen asleep. But if we judged ourselves, we would not come under judgment. When we are judged by the Lord, we are being disciplined so that we will not be condemned with the world.* —1 Corinthians 11:27-32

If we place ourselves in the position of judge, we are in trouble. Don't be fooled into being an accuser by judging others, when we ourselves need a defender. It is not our position to bring people to account for their sins. We may be called to bring correction, if we are able to help in that way, but our place is to intercede on their behalf— it is the job of the Holy Spirit to convict.

> *And a servant of the Lord must not quarrel but be gentle to all, able to teach, patient, in humility correcting those who are in opposition, if God perhaps will grant them repentance, so that they may know the truth, and that they may come to their senses and escape the snare of the devil, having been taken captive by him to do his will.* —2 Timothy 2:24-26

Another deception

Sometimes intercessors feel that if they are under attack they must be doing something right. The enemy loves to hear this; it gives him glory. It keeps the saint who is under attack from examining why this is happening, and take for granted that this is a part of spiritual warfare.

After this happens enough times, I have seen intercessors drop out of the battle saying, "I just can't take the fight anymore." They often develop a fear of any type of prayer. But, even though they don't engage in intercession, things don't get better for them because the root of the problem wasn't discovered. Some have even moved into unbelief and no longer have faith that the Blood of Jesus is capable of overcoming principalities and power. They haven't come to the understanding that they didn't present their prayers correctly. Their case was lost due to a technicality, which could have been that they didn't go to court and get the legal rights removed from the enemy. It could be that they fought incorrectly and opened a door for the enemy to come through and attack them or their family.

There is a *major difference* between saying "I come against you evil spirit," or "I come against you spirit of abortion (or any principality or power)," and presenting a petition correctly before the Righteous Judge.

If we, or our family, are being attacked consistently, we should examine our warfare to see if there is another way to fight. The Lord doesn't want His children hurt. He is well able to protect us and longs to defend us.

None of us are above being deceived

As we stand before Jesus, who is the Living Word, a bright light will shine forth as our case is moved into grace and mercy, and His light will expose all lies and we will see the truth. We see an example of this light that exposes hidden sin found in the story about Paul.

Paul was a rabbi and a teacher of rabbis, a scholar of the Word and very respected as a religious leader. But he was blinded by the spirit of religion, and didn't know it. We see in Acts 9:4-14 that God had to physically intervene and show Paul his blindness by actually striking him blind. It was a symbolic act to demonstrate to him that he was seeing things incorrectly. When the scales (or veils) came off, it changed Paul's life completely.

When the light of God shone down on Paul, a voice spoke out of the light calling him by name. He revealed to Paul that he had been working against God, not for God as Paul had believed. Up to that point he thought he was helping God, but the truth was that he was deceived by satan. He had something like scales over his eyes. I believe this represented that his mind had been blinded or covered over; his mind had been veiled by a lie. None of us are above being deceived.

I believe the intercessors of that day were crying out to God to make an intervention on their behalf, targeting Paul in their prayers. He was the one they were so frightened of because he was rounding them up and throwing them in prison. He was present at the stoning of Stephen, a believer, and approved of his murder.

Paul did all of this in the name of God, defending God (he thought) from these occult type people; that is how he looked at them. He was in conflict with the will of the Lord and he didn't know it. He was sinning against the Lord, but when the truth was made clear to him, he repented and asked forgiveness, and was baptized to prove his total conversion as a believer in Jesus Christ.

Paul, himself, prayed for us as believers in Ephesians 1:18, that the eyes of our understanding would be enlightened. In Romans 12:2, he told us to be transformed by the renewing of our minds.

Is there a veil over your eyes?

As you are reading this, you may be wondering if there is an area where a veil (which has created a spiritual barrier) has been cast over the eyes of your understanding. One way to tell is if you find yourself dealing with the same problems again and again. Seek the Lord; He has prepared a way for you to be free. He is waiting for you in the Courtroom. The Courtroom can be an altar at your church, or on your knees in your home. The Courtroom is where He will reveal truth and expose lies. He is looking for the opportunity to set you free.

Of course, we can't use this as an antidote for willful disobedience, with the idea, 'I will sin and then ask for forgiveness.' This isn't true repentance — both God and the enemy know this. This scripture in Matthew is addressing believers who may possibly have tried this.

> *Not everyone who says to me, "Lord. Lord," will enter the Kingdom of Heaven, but only he who does the will of my father who is in heaven. Many will say to me on that day, "Lord, Lord, did we not prophesy in your name, and in your name drive out demons and perform many miracles?" Then I will tell them plainly, I never knew you. Away from me you evildoers!* —Matthew 7:21-23 NIV

We are each responsible for our walk with the Lord. Don't follow anyone's teaching blindly; research everything for yourself and don't take anything for granted that you are taught from any pulpit. These are perilous times. It won't work on the Day of Judgment to say, "But so and so taught me this. I didn't know it didn't agree with your Word."

Guard your eyes

Here is a testimony concerning how what we look at can be a trap of the enemy, and how it can affect us.

As a Christian, I knew it was sin to move into my boyfriend's home. I had many wrong motives and I justified each one. Months went by and everything seemed to be going all right. I was living in deception and a false sense of happiness. The entire time, the enemy and the spirit of witchcraft were at work. My boyfriend was steeped in the occult through the computer and DVD games. I was in this environment that I now know opened me up to curses.

Prior to living with him, I could fall to sleep as soon as a movie would come on. While living with him I would nap on the love seat while he played these computer games. The game that he liked the most had sci-fi characters that would shoot fiery darts of white and black magic. One of the darts was to "arrest sleep" in the opponent. Since the week he started playing this game, I began having severe trouble going, and staying asleep. I started to play a very common, "innocent" computer game called "Jewel Quest". The screen had a jewel grid with a stone idol on it. I noticed that after playing this game for several weeks I felt an oppression come upon me. I would describe the feeling as a stone-like feeling in my mind. There was a horrible, hopeless feeling of my mind turning to stone. After a while, I broke up with this guy and did not live with him any longer. I renewed my relationship with the Lord but the demons I had allowed in, stayed with me.

I had not been able to take a nap or go to sleep at night without medication for eight months. It was horrible. The effect of sleep deprivation was devastating. I was hospitalized three times and was very harassed mentally, emotionally and physically.

After nine months of this, I went to the home of Jeanette Strauss. I shared my dilemma with her and she counseled me. We prayed together and took my case into the Courtroom of Heaven, which I had never heard of before. I repented and asked forgiveness for my sins. I asked that the Lord would remove the legal rights of this enemy that was attacking me, and deliver me of these two demons and anyone else that was with them. I felt them leave. Then I asked that the Lord to move me from the Courtroom of Judgment into the Throne Room of Grace and Mercy. Boy, the veil came off the eyes of my understanding. I felt it go immediately!

I have not had a bit of trouble sleeping since that time, and the mind thing is gone for good. Now I really understand how deadly this type of seduction can be. It almost succeeded in killing me. On a lighter note, as soon as we concluded our Courtroom prayers and said amen, a very loud voice yelled "I am free! I am free!" We looked at each other shocked—then burst into laughter as I remembered that it was the call tone for messages on my phone that was going off in my coat pocket!

Praying always with all prayer and supplication in the Spirit, being watchful to this end with all perseverance and supplication for all the saints.

Ephesians 6:18

Chapter Eight

The Ambassador of Reconciliation

Position and protocol in the Courtroom

Intercession is when one person stands before God on behalf of another. In our position as intercessors, we become Ambassadors of Reconciliation. We enter the Courtroom equipped with the legal power of attorney given to us by Jesus to act on His behalf as His ambassador on the earth. We are co- councilors with Him.

As believers, we are New Testament priests of the Lord and are considered eligible to offer intercession on behalf of God's people. This is much like the Old Testament priests did, except we receive our forgiveness for sin from the sacrificial shed blood of our Savior Jesus Christ.

And from Jesus Christ, the faithful witness, the firstborn from the dead, and the ruler over the kings of the earth. To Him who loved us and washed us from our sins in His own blood, and has made us kings and priests to His God and Father, to Him be glory and dominion forever and ever. Amen. —Revelation 1:5-6

The emphasis of our work is not on us. The responsibility of the outcome of our Courtroom intercession is on Jesus. We are merely the go-between. As intercessors we represent Jesus. We become His voice on the earth and in the Courtroom of Heaven.

We are merely the go-between. God calls us to intercede for others, to contend in agreement with Him. Contend: Hebrew # 1777: to rule, by implication. To judge (as umpire) also to strive (as at law) contend, execute judgment, judge, minister judgment, plead (the cause) at strife, strive.

So we are Christ's ambassadors, God making His appeal as it were through us. We [as Christ's personal representatives] beg you for His sake to lay hold of the divine favor [now offered you] and be reconciled to God. For our sake He made Christ [virtually] to be sin Who knew no sin, so that in and through Him we might become [endued with, viewed as being in, and examples of] the righteousness of God [what we ought to be, approved and acceptable and in right relationship with Him, by His goodness]. —2 Corinthians 5:20-21 AMP.

"I, even I, am He who blots out your transgressions for My own sake; And I will not remember your sins. Put Me in remembrance; Let us contend together; State your case, that you may be acquitted. —Isaiah 43:25-26

Because of our own testimony of life experiences we learn to view others with compassion instead of judgment. In our position as Ambassadors of Reconciliation, we are very important to the person or situation we are representing. It is important for us too, for as we bless others we will be blessed.

And the LORD turned the captivity of Job, when he prayed for his friends: the LORD gave Job twice as much as he had before.
—Job 42:10

An ambassador is a representative of a government. As ambassadors for Jesus Christ, we represent the government of God. There are specific God-given laws that govern the kingdom of heaven. We will be looking at laws of liberty, not legalism or man-made religious laws but spiritual legal strategies that will help believers live a more victorious life.

We can be thankful that, as humble intercessors, we aren't required to have expertise or training in the earthly legal system to present a case in the Courtroom of Heaven. The Holy Spirit says He will direct our mouths as to what to say when we are presenting our case.

For I will give you a mouth and a wisdom which all of your adversaries will not be able to contradict or resist. —Luke 21:15

The Lord is the God of redemption and reconciliation. He has many different ways to redeem a person from the clutches of the enemy. One way would be through the prayers of an intercessor, an Ambassador of Reconciliation, who is equipped with the legal power of attorney given by Jesus Christ to act on His behalf.

He will even deliver one who is not innocent; Yes, he will be delivered by the purity of your hands. Job 22:30 NKJV.

As an Ambassador, our goal through prayer is to:

To open their eyes, and to turn them from darkness to light, and from the power of satan unto God, that they may receive forgiveness of sins, and inheritance among them which are sanctified by faith that is in me. —Acts 16:18

As we stand in the gap, repenting on behalf of the person's sin committed against God, asking for forgiveness and a time of grace so they may come to their senses, God moves. An example of this identification repentance is found in Daniel in chapter 9, especially verse 20.

And while I was speaking and praying, and confessing my sin and the sin of my people Israel, and presenting my supplication before the Lord my God for the Holy Mountain of my God.

God heard and honored this prayer of identification repentance on behalf of a nation, how much more as we cry out for mercy on behalf of people trapped in bondages. Don't let the enemy rob you of your peace over what is happening, or what might appear to be out of control. Decreeing God's Word releases power into the situation, to bring about supernatural miraculous deliverances.

Intercessors legislating from the heavenlies

In the physical realm, legislators are elected officials. They have the authority to make, enact or repeal laws. Intercessors are legislators in the kingdom of God, who have been elected by Him. When we intercede in the Courtroom of Heaven to get a law overturned, we are to petition for a new law to take its place. An example would be, pulling down the stronghold or altar of abortion (representing murder and death), and speaking life over the city and state, reestablishing the law of God that says, "You shall not murder."

When it comes to other ungodly laws/strongholds, after intercessors stand in the gap repenting and asking for forgiveness, which pulls down the strongholds, it is important to replace that old stronghold. We dethrone the enemy and enthrone the Lord over the city or region. Speak scriptural blessings over your city or situation. Speaking the blessing will build an altar to the Lord to fill the place where there was once a stronghold that had a curse attached. This removes the legal cause that allows a curse to come (Proverbs 2:26).

What about strongholds?

At this point, I know some are asking about how this relates to pulling down strongholds. Strongholds are areas in a believer's or unbeliever's mind where satan and his demon spirits have authority because of sin, or because a person believes a lie about themselves that is contrary to the Word. The scripture instructs us to pull down those strongholds in our minds.

For the weapons of our warfare are not carnal but mighty in God for pulling down strongholds, casting down arguments and every high thing that exalts itself against the knowledge of God, bringing every thought into captivity to the obedience of Christ, and being ready to punish all disobedience when your obedience is fulfilled. — 2 Corinthians 10:4-6

Strongholds are first established in the mind (our will and emotions) also called the soul realm, and then develop into actions. This is why we are to take every thought captive. Behind a stronghold is a lie, a place of personal bondage where God's Word has been subjugated to any unscriptural idea or personally confused belief that is held to be true. Behind every lie is a fear, and behind every fear is an idol. Idols are established wherever there is a failure to trust in the provisions of God that are ours through Jesus Christ. *(Commentary)*

The main weapon used to pull down these strongholds is God's Word.

For the word of God is living and powerful, and sharper than any two-edged sword, piercing even to the division of soul and spirit, and of joints and marrow, and is a discerner of the thoughts and intents of the heart. —Hebrews 4:12

We have to remove these strongholds by dealing with changing the minds of the people through intercession. An example would be the stronghold of the spirit of pornography. First, we go into the Courtroom repenting for ourselves. Then we repent on behalf of those caught up in this sin, and ask for forgiveness. We then ask the Lord to extend grace and mercy as He works in their lives. He will orchestrate circumstances in the person's life, and give them dreams and visions, or even speak directly to them to enable them to come into alignment with His will for their life.

Coming against principalities in our cities

Curses over nations or cities can come through principalities and powers who, due to sin, have been allowed to place a curse on an area, and they have obtained the legal right to do so. Therefore, the spirit of death becomes a plague on the city or area of its jurisdiction.

Like a flitting sparrow, like a flying swallow, So a curse without cause shall not alight. —Proverbs 26:2

A curse is subject to the Word, which is forced to give permission when sin can be cited as its cause. The way the intercessors can know what to target in prayer and supplication is by researching statistics that result in the symptoms the state or city exhibits. The internet is a good source of information. For instance, the spirit of abortion would have symptoms that would include teenage suicide, and murders. It could include divorces, which is the death of a marriage—anything that would come under the heading of death related incidents, especially of children and young adults. After repenting and asking forgiveness for any personal sin we may have committed against the Lord, we can bring our petition before the Judge to include the breaking of a curse of death over the area.

If the state law makes it legal to perform abortions, then the principality has every legal right to be operating. He has gained authority to punish, including the parents and the children, to the point of bringing death to those who live in the state that legalized the death of the unborn. The people who voted this in have rejected God's Word, which says; "You shall not murder." Therefore, an intercessor wouldn't have the legal authority to bind the enemy until someone stands in the gap and repents on behalf of the sin being committed within the state. According to the Word, the intercessor would have to repent for the sins, ask forgiveness, and ask the Lord to move the state into the Throne Room of Grace and Mercy.

There is more work to be done than to just say the words, "I command the curse to be broken over this state, in the name of Jesus," and rebuke and bind the enemy. In prayer, we sometimes ask that anyone involved with agreeing with the spirit we are dealing with, will have a 'Damascus Road' visitation experience from the Lord, as Paul did in Acts 9.

If the case was being tried in the earthly realm, you would be the intercessor representing your state. You would bring a petition to the judge because you want to get the principality and power of abortion removed from your state. The accuser (who is usually the prosecuting attorney) now takes on the role of the defense attorney. He is there to defend the legal rights of his client, the spirit of abortion. He will present his evidence, which would be the written state law that has been voted on and put in place by the people. He might even show how much the state gives to Planned Parenthood to fund these abortions.

Then your turn comes to present your evidence. What do you have to refute his claim? You don't have an argument because he is showing evidence of a state law in place that gives this spirit its legal right to operate in its' mission of death. Legally the spirit can operate, not just in the area of abortion, but also in other areas that can bring death within the state. What is the earthly judge to do?

The defense attorney (satan) has worked in the hearts of the people to get the laws put in place. Whether or not people have voted for abortion, they are still affected spiritually under a corporate guilt that encompasses the state and region. At least if you voted against that law, it would be a testimony in your favor. The defense attorney is thrilled that he was successful in getting this law put in place, and now he has been able to get you bound by the law so you can't actively affect his kingdom, at least in this area. The truth is that he can't remove this spirit even if he wanted to; the heavenly Judge is the only one who can give the order to remove a spirit. This spirit belongs to the enemy's kingdom—the kingdom of darkness. For him to even try to evict it would be to divide his kingdom against itself, and then his kingdom would fall. He is prideful, and calculating but not foolish in most cases. Don't underestimate your enemy.

But He, [well] aware of their intent and purpose, said to them, Every kingdom split up against itself is doomed and brought to desolation, and so house falls upon house. [The disunited household will collapse.] And if Satan also is divided against himself, how will his kingdom last? For you say that I expel demons with the help of and by Beelzebub. —Luke 11:17-18 AMP

If you were to get angry about it and, in your frustration, begin to challenge the defense attorney and say, "I bind you; I rebuke you and command you to leave, in the name of Jesus," what will that prove? You would be out of order. The defense attorney will object and maybe ask the judge to remove you from the courtroom. You would be handed over to the security officer and taken to jail. The judge may have to charge you with contempt of court.

Courtroom protocol

We see an example in Jude, about a conversation between Michael the Archangel and satan. Michael knew protocol and adhered to it. We see that he guarded his attitude and tone of voice as he dealt with satan.

But when [even] the archangel Michael, contending with the devil, judicially argued (disputed) about the body of Moses, he dared not [presume to] bring an abusive condemnation against him, but [simply] said, The Lord rebuke you! But these men revile (scoff and sneer at) anything they do not happen to be acquainted with and do not understand; and whatever they do understand physically [that which they know by mere instinct], like irrational beasts--by these they corrupt themselves and are destroyed (perish). —Jude 1:9-10 AMP

This scripture could describe a person who, when praying, comes against satan or his cohorts unlawfully, because of a lack of knowledge concerning the legal rights of these spiritual dignitaries. It is not our position to ridicule or be condescending toward our opponent.

A story that speaks of these principalities being over areas and how to deal with them, is found in Daniel Chapter 10. Daniel is interceding on behalf of his sinful nation. He doesn't address the principalities, but addresses the Judge. He repents and asking forgiveness for the sins against God. He prayed for 21 days before getting an answer. He had an angelic encounter, and the angel Gabriel, told him that his prayer of repentance had been heard by the Lord from the first day, but that he had been delayed because he was involved in a battle with a principality over another country. It reinforces the fact that our battle isn't against flesh and blood but is indeed against forces we cannot see.

We can remind the Lord of the intercession of Abraham for the city of Sodom. The Lord listened to Abraham's appeals on behalf of

Sodom. Time and again he requested mercy for the city. His final plea was that if ten righteous men could be found in the city, would God spare it? The Lord said He would not destroy the wicked city if there were but ten righteous men found there. Ten righteous men couldn't be found, so the city was destroyed (Genesis 18). The Lord does not want to destroy our state. He loves the people and He has a prophetic destiny for us to fulfill. He is willing to extend mercy, if we will ask.

It is up to the intercessor to intercede before the Judge in the Courtroom of Heaven and follow His instructions to get this law changed. The intercessor, who is the Ambassador of Reconciliation, must present a petition—an appeal on behalf of the people, repenting for sin, asking forgiveness, and requesting a season of grace and mercy. During this time of grace and mercy, the Judge can remove the veil from the eyes of the understanding of the people of the state. They will see truth, and by His grace, with the help of the Holy Spirit, He will enable them to get the law overturned. We can also remind Him of His word spoken over Jerusalem.

Run to and fro through the streets of Jerusalem; see now and know; and seek in her open places if you can find a man, If there is anyone who executes judgment, who seeks the truth, and I will pardon her. — Jeremiah 5:1

God's idea of executing judgment is to extend grace and mercy after repentance. Reconciliation and pardon is His desire. Satan's plan of executing judgment is to steal, kill, and destroy.

Another testimony about our city

We had a problem in our city, which was jokingly referred to as the 'revolving door' in our county jail. We prepared to go into the Courtroom by gathering statistics of arrest records that showed us the symptoms of the root causes, the reasons people were in jail. We stood in the gap, repented and asked forgiveness over the root causes of those symptoms. We asked the Judge to set these captives free at a spiritual level, so they would get free physically. We asked that He would use the jail as a revival center. We then decreed that the gates of hell over the jail would be closed, and the gates of heaven would be opened over the jail. We spoke blessings over the jail.

Within six weeks, there was a changing of the guards in the staff of the jail ministry. People retired who had been in charge for many years. There was nothing wrong with these servants of the Lord, but new ministers of the gospel came in with fresh teachings and formats, and the number of those being saved increased. Outside programs were put in place to follow up with those who got saved. More people got involved in jail ministry and we began to hear of revival in the jail! For the past two years, the number of parolees returning to jail has steadily been on the decrease. This will change our city.

The other thing we did to help our city was to start a citywide prayer meeting through Aglow International. As we were searching for a place to have our Aglow meetings, we checked out our municipal building to see if they had a room available. They said that they did and, because Aglow is a tax exempt organization, we could meet there for free. The only room available just happened to be the actual council chambers! So we scheduled our meeting once a month, just ahead of theirs. We took our city into the Courtroom of Heaven and turned the council chambers and the decisions being made over to the Lord's will. This is just an idea for those who have citywide prayer in their hearts. Any room in the city municipal building would have worked. It was certainly symbolic that it was in the exact location where the governing force would be meeting to make decisions that would have a direct impact on our city and its people.

If you are interested in starting a prayer meeting for your city thru Aglow International, information is available at www.aglowinternational.org.

Stay under His protection

To be protected, we must conduct warfare properly. The Lord speaks of a spiritual battle where the person underestimates and makes light of his enemy and pays the price for it. Satan is called 'Leviathan' in this scripture.

"Can you draw out Leviathan with a hook, Or snare his tongue with a line which you lower? Can you put a reed through his nose, Or pierce his jaw with a hook? Will he make many supplications to you? Will he speak softly to you? Will he make a covenant with you? Will you take him as a servant forever? Will you play with him as with a bird, Or will you leash him for your maidens? Will your companions make a banquet of him? Will they apportion him among the merchants? Can you fill his skin with harpoons, Or his head with fishing spears? Lay your hand on him; Remember the battle—Never do it again! —Job. 41:1-8

When we look at examples of how spiritual warfare was conducted throughout the Old Testament, the first thing they did was to repent. They realized their sin because they were being defeated on every front. They humbled themselves before the Lord, repented, and asked forgiveness. Then they would remind the Lord of what He had said in His Word about them—good prophetic words. They would take care of their business in the Courtroom of Heaven first, to get their victory on the earth.

Without a doubt, the Lord required that they fight the battles against their enemies in such a way that He would get the glory. That means they usually were outnumbered, overwhelmed, unprepared, and usually full of fear. But through humility and repentance, often the Lord did all the fighting and defeated their enemies. Sometimes all they had to do to put their enemy on the run were symbolic, things like blowing a shofar, and holding up a lamp and shouting. Sometimes it was to sing songs of praise as the Heavenly Hosts of the Lord wiped out their enemies.

Therefore He is also able to save to the uttermost those who come to God through Him, since He always lives to make intercession for them.
Hebrews 7:25

Chapter Nine

Defense Attorney — Our Advocate

Fortunately for the believer, we have an Advocate present in the Courtroom. Scripture clearly tells us that Jesus is our Advocate and is continually interceding for us.

> *Therefore He is also able to save to the uttermost those who come to God through Him, since He always lives to make intercession for them. —Hebrews 7:25*

> *My little children, these things write I unto you, that ye sin not. And if any man sin, we have an advocate with the Father, Jesus Christ the righteous: And he is the propitiation for our sins: and not for ours only, but also for the sins of the whole world. And hereby we do know that we know him, if we keep his commandments. —1 John 2:1*

> *Seeing then that we have a great High Priest Who has passed through the heavens, Jesus the Son of God; let us hold fast our confession. For we do not have a high priest who cannot sympathize with our weaknesses, but was in all points tempted as we are, yet without sin. Let us therefore come boldly to the Throne of Grace that we may obtain Mercy and find Grace to help in time of need. —Hebrews 4:14-16*

An advocate is one who pleads another's cause before a judge; he is the counsel for the defense.

Advocate: (1) comforter, parakletos {summoned, called to one's side, esp. called to one's aid, one who pleads another's cause before a judge, a pleader, counsel for defense, legal assistant, an advocate. (2) one who pleads another's cause with one, an intercessor. Jesus is sitting at God's right hand, pleading with God the Father for the pardon of our sins. In the widest sense, a helper, aider, assistant.

> *So we are Christ's ambassadors, God making His appeal as it were through us. We [as Christ's personal representatives] beg you for His sake to lay hold of the divine favor [now offered you] and be reconciled to God. For our sake He made Christ [virtually] to be sin Who knew no sin, so that in and through Him we might become [endued with, viewed as being in, and examples of] the righteousness of God [what we ought to be, approved and acceptable and in right relationship with Him, by His goodness]. —2 Corinthians 5:20-21 AMP*

Without Jesus as our Advocate, a believer who is in some sort of sin is both the witness and his own defense attorney. In the heavenly Courtroom, you don't get an attorney to act on your behalf unless you petition Jesus to be your Defense Attorney. A person who is knowingly in sin usually won't seek Him as their Defense Attorney. This is a big mistake. Don't run from God when you are in sin, run to Him. He is there waiting for you and has made provision for you to win your case.

Chapter Ten

Secret Weapon Against the Accuser

When I am presenting a case, before I ask the Lord to move the person or situation into the Throne Room of Grace and Mercy, I am often moved to speak in my heavenly prayer language.

This language is the secret weapon the Lord desires for each of His children. This heavenly language bypasses our reasoning and our emotions and brings us the council of the Holy Spirit. He helps us in our petition to the Judge on behalf of a person or situation. This will make the accuser very nervous. He is fearful of a saint who prays in tongues, especially in the Courtroom.

Praying in tongues might not be for the other person or situation, even though that is our focus. It might be intercession of the Holy Spirit on behalf of the one praying. The Lord might have a surprise and want you to ask something of Him that you hadn't thought of before. This revelation may come as you ask Him for the interpretation of your tongues.

Likewise the Spirit also helps in our weaknesses. For we do not know what we should pray for as we ought, but the Spirit Himself makes intercession for us with groanings which cannot be uttered. Now He who searches the hearts knows what the mind of the Spirit is, because He makes intercession for the saints according to the will of God. And we know that all things work together for good to those who love God, to those who are the called according to His purpose. —Romans 8:26-28

If you haven't experienced the promised baptism of the Holy Spirit spoken of in the New Testament, this might be your time to receive.

And Peter answered them, Repent (change your views and purpose to accept the will of God in your inner selves instead of rejecting it) and be baptized, every one of you, in the name of Jesus Christ for the forgiveness of and release from your sins; and you shall receive the gift of the Holy Spirit. —Acts 2:38 AMP

And they were all filled (diffused throughout their souls) with the Holy Spirit and began to speak in other (different, foreign) languages (tongues), as the Spirit kept giving them clear and loud expression [in each tongue in appropriate words]. —Acts 2:4 AMP

If you haven't received this gift of the Holy Spirit, with the evidence of speaking with other tongues, you can pray and ask for this gift. If you have received this gift in the past but have stopped speaking in tongues, you can ask to be filled again. The Holy Spirit will be pleased.

Your prayer could go something like this:

Dear Lord Jesus, I come before you in thanksgiving and praise. Thank You for the gifts You have prepared for me. As I come into Your presence and stand before You, I ask that You will bless me with every one of Your gifts. I am here especially to receive the gift of the infilling of the Holy Spirit with the manifestation of speaking in other tongues.

I repent for any sins I have committed against You and I ask Your forgiveness. I forgive every person who has ever hurt me. I give to you all bitterness, anger and anything else that could block the flow of Your Holy Spirit through me. I ask that as I give You the bitterness and anger and any hindrances that You reveal to me, there will be a divine exchange, and You will come upon me as You came upon the disciples in Acts 2:4, when they all began to speak in other tongues. Thank You, Jesus.

Now begin to speak in other tongues. It may seem like the babbling of a baby, but keep on. For some, it helps to begin to sing a favorite worship song and, after a few sentences, stop singing in English.

Another way to receive your tongues is to pray with another believer who speaks in tongues. After praying the prayer of repentance, begin to speak the words they are speaking in their heavenly language. It may seem awkward at first, but it will loosen your tongue. As you follow along, have the person increase their speed. It won't be long before you notice that you are speaking in your own heavenly language.

I have never seen this fail. I have prayed this way with dozens of people over the years and not one of these people left the session speaking in the same tongue as mine. Once they were launched, the Holy Spirit gave them their own special language.

Some of the people I have prayed with, after they received their own heavenly language, have told me that they had tried for years to receive but hadn't been able to. They said that they had been taught that they shouldn't repeat anyone else's tongues. And when they would pray with others who were praying in tongues, while they were trying to get theirs, they were afraid of repeating the other person's language. When I asked why they weren't supposed to repeat what the other person was saying, they said they didn't know, they were only following what they had been told.

One time while ministering, I asked for anyone to come forward who hadn't received the baptism of the Holy Spirit and wanted to receive the manifestation of speaking in tongues. As we began to lay hands on the people and as they began to receive their tongues, the faith level in the room grew thick and glorious. To my surprise, the pastor came up and asked me to pray for him to receive the baptism. He said that he had tried for years to receive his tongues but couldn't seem to get them. He would pray for others to receive theirs and they would.

As we went into prayer for him, the Holy Spirit spoke to me and said to tell him to repeat his wife's heavenly language after her. I gave him the message. He looked surprised but agreed to try it. She began to speak in tongues and he began to slowly repeat what she said. Within a minute, he was praying in his own language, and not quietly! The next day he confessed he had always been told not to repeat someone else's tongues. He believed that this had blocked him from receiving his own heavenly language.

If speaking in other tongues is praise to the Lord as the Word says, then I would think two people saying the same words would be the same as the church body singing a worship or praise song together. When I asked the Holy Spirit about this He said, "How do you teach a child to learn to talk?" I said, "Have them repeat after us." He said, "That's right".

I am not saying the Holy Spirit isn't capable of baptizing a believer by Himself, because He does that all the time without the help of man. This is just for those who have had a difficult time receiving their heavenly language.

Here is another scripture describing this experience as the believers received the gift of the Holy Spirit.

And the believers from among the circumcised [the Jews] who came with Peter were surprised and amazed, because the free gift of the Holy Spirit had been bestowed and poured out largely even on the Gentiles, For they heard them talking in [unknown] tongues (languages) and extolling and magnifying God. Then Peter asked, Can anyone forbid or refuse water for baptizing these people, seeing that they have received the Holy Spirit just as we have? — Acts 10:45-47 (AMP) (Also see Acts 2:1-18)

If you have further questions or would like to read more about being filled with the Holy Spirit and speaking in other tongues, I would highly recommend the following books: *They Speak With Other Tongues* by John Sherrill and *Nine O'clock in the Morning* by Dennis Bennett.

When we are afraid, we can use another one of our Spiritual secret weapons to scare the spirit of fear so he will flee.

Another tactic the enemy will use is fear. If he is attacking you with fear, this next story may be of help. This testimony isn't shared to make light of anyone's torment because of circumstances they may be in, but hopefully this can be used as a strategy to bring relief from a spirit of fear.

Some years ago, I was asked by my Pastor to lead a group of women in our church to perform a dance in front of a very large gathering of different churches in our city. I was the only one who had experience in this type of ministry, but they learned the dance and we were gathered ready to go before the assembly to dance.

A spirit of fear began to intimidate them. On by one I began to hear things like; "I bind you fear!" "I rebuke you fear"! Other confessions like, "I am so afraid I am going to forget my part and mess it all up," and other negative oaths over themselves. So I gathered everyone to pray. I asked the Lord for a solution for the fear that was attacking them. The Holy Spirit told me to invite the spirit of fear to come along and worship and praise with us.

I shared this with them and we all burst into laughter, and you could just about hear the door slam as that spirit of fear left!

I have another testimony about this spirit of fear. I was in Israel staying with a friend's mother. One day I decided to walk down to the corner grocery store for some ice cream. As soon as I turned out of her gate onto the sidewalk and began to walk down this nice, peaceful, tree lined street I suddenly felt the atmosphere turn antagonistic. I felt a very dark presence descend on me, and fear rose up quickly to attack me.

I had never had this happen in quite this way in my whole life, and suddenly I could just about taste fear! I immediately thought about turning around to run back to the apartment, but right on the heels of that thought, as I cried out to the Lord, came the memory of the time the spirit of fear attacked the dance team.

I collected my thoughts and said aloud, "Well, hello fear. I recognize you, and I am glad you came along. You are just in time to join me as I sing praises to the Lord Jesus. I immediately began to sing,"Oh the blood of Jesus, oh the blood of Jesus, oh the blood of Jesus that washes white as snow!" After the very first 'blood of Jesus', that spirit of fear was gone and he didn't dare come back!

Chapter Eleven

The Battle is God's!

After the showdown with Pharaoh, Moses led the people out of Egypt to the edge of the Red Sea. They had seen the hand of the Lord deliver them supernaturally through the plagues. Now they faced drowning—but God had deliverance in mind. He instructed Moses to hold his staff over the water and command it to part (Genesis 14:16). It parted and the people were delivered from their enemies. They only had to follow God's directions and He did the rest. Obedience was the key.

> *[Urged on] by faith the people crossed the Red Sea as [though] on dry land, but when the Egyptians tried to do the same thing they were swallowed up [by the sea]. Because of faith the walls of Jericho fell down after they had been encompassed for seven days [by the Israelites].*
> *—Hebrews 11:29-30 AMP*

Judges Chapters 6 and 7 tell of when the Angel of the Lord came to Gideon to tell him that the people were in bondage because they had been worshipping foreign gods. The Lord assured him that it was His desire that His people would be victorious over their enemies.

The Angel of the Lord instructed Gideon to physically tear down the altars of Baal belonging to his father, then build an altar to the Lord. He had to deal with the sin of idolatry to gain a victory over the foreign god (or principality). Tearing down the altar was his way of demonstrating repentance on behalf of his city and his generational bloodline. He then offered another sacrifice as his way of repenting for himself.

Then the Lord put Gideon through a series of tests to remove any hope he might have concerning a victory based on the strength of man. The Lord had him go into the battle with their main weapons being symbolic ones: shofars and lamps. The Lord and His hosts fought the battle and the enemies of the Hebrew people ran for their lives. Their victory was complete.

Another great story about the Lord fighting the battle on behalf of His people is in 2 Chronicles, where a large enemy force came against King Jehoshaphat. This story reveals the right protocol for fighting our enemy and how the Lord works on our behalf.

The enemy came against Judah and the first thing Jehoshaphat did was seek the Lord. First, they fasted and repented before the Lord.

After this, the Moabites, the Ammonites, and with them the Meunites came against Jehoshaphat to battle. Then Jehoshaphat feared, and set himself [determinedly, as his vital need] to seek the Lord; he proclaimed a fast in all Judah. And Judah gathered together to ask help from the Lord; even out of all the cities of Judah they came to seek the Lord [yearning for Him with all their desire].

Then Jehoshaphat cried out to the Lord and reminded Him of His promises to them.

And Jehoshaphat stood in the assembly of Judah and Jerusalem in the house of the Lord before the new court And said, O Lord, God of our fathers, are You not God in heaven? And do You not rule over all the kingdoms of the nations? In

Your hand are power and might, so that none is able to withstand You. Did not You, O our God, drive out the inhabitants of this land before Your people Israel and give it forever to the descendants of Abraham Your friend?

He asked for God's help.

O our God, will You not exercise judgment upon them? For we have no might to stand against this great company that is coming against us. We do not know what to do, but our eyes are upon You. And all Judah stood before the Lord, with their children and their wives.

The prophet of the Lord spoke God's answer to them.

Then the Spirit of the Lord came upon Jahaziel son of Zechariah, the son of Benaiah, the son of Jeiel, the son of Mattaniah, a Levite of the sons of Asaph, in the midst of the assembly. He said, Hearken, all Judah, you inhabitants of Jerusalem, and you King Jehoshaphat.

The Lord says this to you: Be not afraid or dismayed at this great multitude; for the battle is not yours, but God's. You shall not need to fight in this battle; take your positions, stand still, and see the deliverance of the Lord [Who is] with you, O Judah and Jerusalem. Fear not nor be dismayed. Tomorrow go out against them, for the Lord is with you.

Then they praised God for the victory – before they even went out to fight!

Jehoshaphat stood and said, Hear me, O Judah, and you inhabitants of Jerusalem! Believe in the Lord your God and you shall be established; believe and remain steadfast to His prophets and you shall prosper. When he had consulted with the people, he appointed singers to sing to the Lord and praise Him in their holy [priestly] garments as they went out before the army, saying, Give thanks to the Lord, for His mercy and loving-kindness endure forever! And when they began to sing and to praise, the Lord set ambushments against the men of Ammon, Moab, and Mount Seir who had come against Judah, and they were [self-] slaughtered;

God not only brought them the victory, He provided so much of their enemies' spoils, that it took three days to collect everything! Then they had another praise party!

When Jehoshaphat and his people came to take the spoil, they found among them much cattle, goods, garments, and precious things which they took for themselves, more than they could carry away, so much they were three days in gathering the spoil. On the fourth day they assembled in the Valley of Beracah. There they blessed the Lord. So the name of the place is still called the Valley of Beracah [blessing]. —2 Chronicles 20:1-30.

It is important to remember the Words of the Lord in verse 15, "The battle is not yours, but God's." These stories are not unique, but parallel other Old Testament stories about God's supernatural intervention. (See Joshua 6:10-20; 2 Kings 7:3-16, 19-35)

The point that these scriptures make is that if we are in the position of righteousness, the Lord will fight our battles. Our goal is to make sure we are standing in the righteousness of Christ and His shed blood before entering into spiritual warfare. The Word speaks of our Christian walk as a battle, and the Lord instructs us to put on spiritual armor.

Finally, my brethren, be strong in the Lord and in the power of His might. Put on the whole armor of God, that you may be able to stand against the wiles of the devil. For we do not wrestle against flesh and blood, but against principalities, against powers, against the rulers of the darkness of this age, against spiritual hosts of wickedness in the heavenly places. Therefore take up the whole armor of God, that you may be able to withstand in the evil day, and having done all, to stand. —Ephesians 6:10-13

Verses 14-17 list the battle dress components of the armor. God tells us to:

Stand therefore, having girded your waist with truth, having put on the breastplate of righteousness, and having shod your feet with the preparation of the gospel of peace; above all, taking the shield of faith with which you will be able to quench all the fiery darts of the wicked one. And take the helmet of salvation, and the sword of the Spirit, which is the word of God;

He instructs us how we are to wrestle the enemy (vs. 18):

Praying always with all prayer and supplication in the Spirit, being watchful to this end with all perseverance and supplication for all the saints.

Perseverance means to be persistent in our prayers. Supplication is a prayer or petition. The word petition is a courtroom term. We can win the battle by taking our case into the Courtroom and the Lord will direct His hosts to fight and defeat our enemy. As we stand firm in our position, the battle will be won.

Here is a scripture with a visual of the heavenly host around God's people.

Then Elisha prayed, Lord, I pray You, open his eyes that he may see. And the Lord opened the young man's eyes, and he saw, and behold, the mountain was full of horses and chariots of fire round about Elisha. —2 Kings 6:17 AMP

As we pray, we establish godly spiritual rule in a situation and, guided by the Holy Spirit, we put in motion angelic hosts to institute His authority in the earthly realm. Every time we follow the instructions of Jesus on how we should pray, we are prophetically decreeing the very thing to happen for those things for which we are praying.

Chapter Twelve

Victim or Victor?

It is strange to think that satan has any legal right to bind a Christian. If we sin against the Word of the Lord, our enemy will take advantage of his legal right to make us his lawful captive.

> *Settle matters quickly with your adversary who is taking you to court. Do it while you are still with him on the way, or he may hand you over to the judge, and the judge may hand you over to the officer, and you may be thrown into prison.*
> *—Matthew 5:25 NIV*

I used to wonder what it meant that I should "settle matters quickly with my adversary." Then, after learning of the Courtroom and how the adversary can take us in to the Courtroom, I had an understanding of this scripture. Now if the enemy should come to me and accuse me of anything, I no longer waste time rebuking or binding him. I immediately go to the Lord and repent and ask forgiveness for any sins I may have committed.

If the enemy wants to torment you or accuse you in any way, don't waste time with him—take it to the Judge and get it settled. This will defeat the demonic accuser, turn the tables on him, and settle the case out of court.

Here is an example:

When you are walking along and the enemy comes and accuses you of a sin from your past that you have already repented and asked forgiveness for, instead of rebuking him, agree with him that you did commit that sin and you remember quite clearly when you repented and asked forgiveness for it. Thank him for reminding you of what the blood of Jesus has done for you. You can encourage him to take his accusation against you for that sin to the Judge. You can be sure he won't.

If he is accusing you of some other sin that you have committed that you haven't yet repented and asked forgiveness, don't rebuke him. Humbly agree with him; don't let him lead you into an argument. Jesus is our example. He never argued with him.

Thank the accuser politely and tell him to stay put so he can be a witness as you repent and ask forgiveness for the sin he is accusing you of, then begin your prayer of repentance, asking forgiveness, and covering it all over with the blood of Jesus. You will turn the tables on him and remove the power he intended to use to bring you before the Judge to get a judgment against you. Just remind him of Romans 8:28.

And we know that all things work together for good to them that love God, to them who are the called according to his purpose.

When the accuser has no authority

Another friend tells of a dream she had after praying for someone and taking them into the Courtroom of Heaven. In the dream, the accuser was standing before the Judge. He was handing the Judge several files with names on them. The Lord asked him what they were and the accuser said, "Judge, these are the records of sins of these particular people." As the Judge looked them over,

He held one of them up and said, "This record has been expunged; destroy this record."

Expunge means to strike out, obliterate, or delete. This is what happens if the enemy tries to bring up an old case that has already been dealt with through repentance and forgiveness. The case is thrown out of court.

But, you must be on the alert! Just because you win your case in court doesn't mean the accuser will leave you alone. When he comes along to remind you of past sins, he opens the door for you to share your testimony with him. Thank him for reminding you of what the blood of Jesus did for you, how the blood of Jesus paid the price for your sin and that your record has been wiped clean. Tell him that, if he doesn't know about the blood of Jesus and what it does for the believer, you will be happy to tell him. This kind of answer is guaranteed to discourage him. He won't come back very often if you deal with him in this way. Even if he does come back, it is great to remind him, and yourself, about what the blood of Jesus does for the believer.

How you become a victim

I can recall times before I learned about the Courtroom, if I didn't agree with someone or a particular viewpoint, I would find myself thinking it over and making decisions that really were judgments based on my opinion. I didn't realize I was guilty of judging a brother.

If the devil spoke in my ear accusing me of judging, I would rebuke him, bind him and command him to go in the name of Jesus. He would shut up, go, and maybe not bother me for a long while. I would feel pretty good about being able to command him to go and know he had left. I would thank the Lord for Jesus and the power of His blood and what He had done for me on the cross. Then I would forget the incident. If I did think about it, quite frankly, I would most likely be prideful about exercising authority over the devil and him having to listen to me and leave. My case of judging another was being tried in the spiritual Courtroom, and I didn't even know it. The enemy must have been getting a good laugh out of my telling him to back off, when I had unknowingly given him a legal right to be there by my judgments. I had a personal experience with this veil of the enemy that covered the eyes of my understanding in the area of judging.

When I worship, I often dance before the Lord. I use adornments and rehearse scripture with them by using interpretive movements. I was dancing with a veil in my hands worshipping the Lord, making a movement that is called 'removing the veil'. As I was spinning and acting out the movement, suddenly the Lord removed the veil that was over the eyes of my understanding that I had no idea was there. I guess you could say something like scales fell from my eyes and I saw His truth.

The Lord spoke to me and said, "You come running into My presence and begin to dance before Me, which I love, but there is a veil between us and you don't even know it" I was shocked. I asked Him, "What veil, Lord?" He said, "You have judged your brother, and therefore I have to judge you!" I said, "Lord, please remind me of the times when I judged wrongly so I can repent for them."

He immediately brought to my mind a ministry that I had been watching on television the day before. They had said something that did not go along with the Word of God, at least not the way I interpreted it. I had turned the channel and said something judgmental about the ministry. Next, he showed me an acquaintance who had asked me for advice and then didn't take the advice, did exactly the opposite, and had gotten into problems because of it. I had judged that person. He showed me several other times of judgment. I am sure I could have been on the floor all day repenting, considering the many occasions I had judged others in my lifetime.

I asked Him if I could just do a blanket repentance for all the times I had been judgmental. I wasn't flippant about it. I realized this could have serious consequences in my life and I had just had a divine visitation to stop me from further deception in this area. It seemed acceptable to pray a prayer of repentance and ask for forgiveness in this area of sin in my life that would cover every time I had judged in the past.

I prayed a prayer of repentance and began to thank the Lord for showing me this sin. But I had one little bit of rebellion left, kind of like a kid who gets reprimanded by a parent and still wants to have the last word. Trying to justify myself I said, "Lord, I thought this was just my opinion, not a judgment". He said, "You can have an opinion and keep it to yourself, but when you shared it with your mother, it became a judgment. Because of your opinion, she judged the ministry that she didn't even know. By telling your mother your opinion, you sold yourself into the hands of the enemy." I quickly repented! Then I called my mother and asked her forgiveness for sharing that, and prayed a prayer of repentance with her so she wouldn't be under judgment.

Therefore you are inexcusable, O man, whoever you are who judge, for in whatever you judge another you condemn yourself; for you who judge practice the same things.
—Romans 2:1

This was a good lesson for me. I realized how very seriously both God and satan take the words that come out of my mouth. By my own words, I am either justified or condemned.

He uses our words and actions to bring about conviction

Look also at ships: although they are so large and are driven by fierce winds, they are turned by a very small rudder wherever the pilot desires. Even so the tongue is a little member and boasts great things. See how great a forest a little fire kindles! —James 3:4-5

The apostle compares the tongue to the rudder of a ship. Although tiny in comparison to the whole structure of the ship, the rudder determines the course that the ship will follow. Used rightly, it will guide the ship safely to its appointed harbor. Used wrongly, it will cause shipwreck. The same is true of the words of our mouth.

The fruit of our tongues can cause a lot of trouble for us. It's sad to say, but for most of us, the enemy doesn't have to work very hard to get dirt on us; he only needs to hang around for a while and listen to what we are saying.

A man's [moral] self shall be filled with the fruit of his mouth; and with the consequence of his words he must be satisfied [whether good or evil]. Death and life are in the power of the tongue, and they who indulge in it shall eat the fruit of it [for death or life]. —Proverbs 18:20-21 AMP

You are snared by the words of your mouth; You are taken by the words of your mouth. —Proverbs 6:2

The words of our mouth are an open gateway for good or evil to enter.

A fool's mouth is his destruction, and his lips are the snare of his soul. —Proverbs 18:7

Set a guard over my mouth, Lord, keep watch over the door of my lips. —Psalms 141:3

God hears what we say. Our words are our testimony. Don't put yourself in the Courtroom by your own words. One of the many sins that satan can us accuse of is when we judge our brother.

But why do you judge your brother? Or why do you show contempt for your brother? For we shall all stand before the judgment seat of Christ. —Romans 14:10

The Lord doesn't want believers to judge their brother, or they will be in danger of judgment.

Do not judge and criticize and condemn others, so that you may not be judged and criticized and condemned yourselves. For just as you judge and criticize and condemn others you will be judged and criticized and condemned and in accordance with the measure you deal out to others it will be dealt out again to you. —Matthew 7:1-2

Refuse to get involved in vain discussions; they always end up in fights. God's servant must not be argumentative, but a gentle listener and a teacher who keeps cool, working firmly but patiently with those who refuse to obey.
—Timothy 2:23-26 MSG

And [when] the people complained, it displeased the LORD: and the LORD heard [it]; and his anger was kindled; Don't hold a grudge. James 5:9 Grudge not one against another, brethren, lest ye be condemned: behold, the judge standeth before the door. —Numbers 11:1,2

May the words of my mouth be pleasing to You O Lord.
—Psalms 119:14

Extend grace to others

God wants to extend mercy, but we can limit Him!

For He shall have judgment without mercy for those who show no mercy. Mercy rejoices against judgment. —James 2:13

Brethren, if a man is overtaken in any trespass, you who are spiritual restore such a one in a spirit of gentleness, considering yourself lest you also be tempted.
—Galatians 6:1

In many cases, a person might blame satan for their problems and be tempted to come against him, when at the root it is God Himself. As the Judge, He is forced to turn a person over to the enemy because sin in their life.

We see this in I Corinthians 5:5:

To deliver such as one unto Satan for the destruction of the flesh, that the spirit may be saved in the day of the Lord Jesus.

Chapter Thirteen

Intercession or Spiritual Warfare?

Once, after teaching in a meeting on the Courtroom, we went into the Courtroom of Heaven in corporate prayer, to repent and ask forgiveness for improper prayers that we may have prayed in the past.

A man, who I later learned had been a government official in the state where I was ministering, spoke out and repented on behalf of leading people in praying unlawful prayers and commanding principalities and powers to do things they didn't have to do because they had the legal authority. He repented for spending so much time addressing the enemy and not going directly to the Judge. He repented and asked forgiveness for any backlash from the enemy he was responsible for, due to his incorrect or lawless way of praying, possibly causing those he led in prayer pain and suffering. It was an emotional time.

After we finished, he said a great burden had lifted from him when he prayed and set the record straight. He said he had felt that, in the past, he had done something wrong in the spiritual realm, crossing a line he shouldn't have crossed, but he hadn't known what it was. His family had been attacked and they were still going through some hard times, but he knew that because it was settled in the Courtroom of Heaven, it was now settled on earth.

This is a prime example of what happens when people go directly into spiritual warfare without first repenting for their sins. I have heard people use the terminology of intercession and spiritual warfare as if they are the same thing. By definition, they are direct opposites. Intercession must come before spiritual warfare.

Intercession is all about reconciliation through the pleading of a case. To intercede is an act between parties with a view to reconciling differences.

When you intercede for someone, you are taking the position of a negotiator, trying to settle differences between two sides. You are not coming against; you are coming on behalf of someone. You are asking the Judge to rule favorably in the case.

Spiritual warfare is all about dominion and fighting. It is an aggressive stepping up offensively against opposing forces. Warfare is defined as open and declared fighting between states or nations. Warfare is a state of hostility, conflict or antagonism, a struggle between opposing forces or for a particular end.

In warfare, there is no reconciliation. It is kill or be killed. Here is an example of intercession going ahead of spiritual warfare.

We see in Chapter 4 in the book of Judges that Israel did evil in the site of the Lord, so He sold them into the hands of their enemy (a picture of the Courtroom). Then the people of Israel cried out to the Lord for help. This is a pattern seen throughout the Word: sin, repent, get forgiven, and be restored to God's favor. It is still the same today; God uses the enemy to bring us to repentance.

At the time, there was a judge in Israel named Deborah, who was also a prophetess. Israel was being defeated by their enemies and cried out to the Lord and God heard them. Deborah received a word from the Lord that it was time for Israel to fight for their freedom. She called for Barak, the commander of Israel's army, and told him it was time to go to war. He trusted her word as a prophetess, but he was fearful. He said if you go with me, I will go. If you won't go with me, I won't go. She responded by saying,

> *"I will surely go with you; nevertheless there will be no glory for you in the journey you are taking, for the LORD will sell Sisera into the hand of a woman." (vs. 9)*

From this, we might think that the victory will come through Deborah. I think most of us can relate to receiving a prophetic word and presuming we have an understanding of the outcome; we might be expecting one thing, but see it fulfilled in a different way.

They went on to fight the battle, defeated their enemies and gained their freedom. A woman named Jael was responsible for killing Sisera, the head of the enemy army. Deborah gives her credit for the fulfillment of the prophetic word. Personally, I think Deborah should have some of the credit. She was the one who exhorted Barak to fight. She was the one who led the people into repentance and worship before the battle (see Judges Chapter 3).

Before they went into battle, Deborah composed a song to lead them, a tribute to the Lord that reads like a personal diary. It begins with the description of how life was in Israel. Village life had ceased in Israel. The highways were deserted because of the fear and oppression that was upon the people. No one would walk along the road for fear of being robbed. She says,

> *The villages were unoccupied and rulers ceased in Israel until you arose--you, Deborah, arose--a mother in Israel. [Formerly] they chose new gods; then war was in the gates. Was there a shield or spear seen among 40,000 in Israel?*
> *—Judges 5:7-8 AMP*

The people had lost their strength and freedom because of the worship of foreign gods. Then she goes on to recount her battle strategy.

Far from the noise of the archers, (front lines of the battle) among the watering places, (places of peace and safety), there they shall recount, the righteous acts of the Lord. (vs. 11)

The 'righteous acts' would be the wonderful things the Lord had done on their behalf before they moved away from Him spiritually. In repentance, they extolled the praises of God. The Word says they rehearsed the acts of the Lord. It goes on to say that after they spent time worshipping the Lord and reminding Him of how he had fought for them in the past, Deborah led the people down to the city gates to fight the war.

This can be symbolic terminology. The war is fought at the city gates in the spiritual realm, even if the actual war is in another location, as in this story. The gates were where all the decisions were made for the city. Verses 19 and 20 speak of heavenly intervention in this battle.

The kings came and fought, then fought the kings of Canaan at Taanach by the waters of Megiddo. Gain of booty they did not obtain. From the heavens the stars fought, from their courses they fought against Sisera.

The angelic host most certainly played an active part in this story because it says the kings took no spoils or silver. These kings could mean human kings or spiritual kings. Angels in charge over Israel wouldn't be interested in spoils. The scripture goes on to say the stars fought from their courses. Some commentaries say this refers to rain, but others say the stars are angels.

When others aren't aware of the protocol

Since I became aware of this Courtroom protocol, I have had opportunities to be trapped by the enemy by judging other intercessors. Because I travel quite a bit in ministry, I am often a part of intercession and spiritual warfare gatherings. I have become sensitive to the way that intercession and spiritual warfare is conducted.

I have been in meetings where the intercession leadership begins to come against principalities and powers, sometimes screaming at them, commanding and rebuking them, binding them, and railing against them, which is contrary to scripture.

For those who have read this book and agree with it, you may wonder how to deal with this. We have to assume that they aren't aware of the correct protocol. When I find myself in this situation, I begin to stand in the gap on behalf of sin committed against the Lord for unlawful prayers, Then I ask the Lord to move everyone from the Courtroom of Judgment to the Throne Room of Grace and Mercy. I ask He place us under His wings, and sometimes I read Psalm 91 out loud as others are shouting.

What part are we to play in bringing revelation to the leadership about the correct way to pray. This is a sensitive issue. Ask the Lord what you are to do. Every case will be different. If this is happening in your church, one suggestion would be to loan this book to the head intercessor or to someone who has the ear of the pastor. Many people give their pastors books to read and the book gets put on the shelf unread because they have other pressing issues to deal with. If you know the head intercessor personally, you could ask if you could make an appointment with them and share your concerns. No matter what you do, it is not your job to accuse or judge anyone of interceding the wrong way. As you extend grace and mercy in this area, others will listen to you.

I realize that there are many intercessors that pray correctly and still get attacked. This can happen even when they are doing everything right. It's just like fighting a physical war on the earth, people get hurt. This is a price that some will pay. But there may be some who are running headlong into battle without the proper preparation of intercession needed to win the victory and stay alive. If you know intercessors that are constantly under fire, don't judge them. The Lord may have given them a special assignment. Pray for them for the mercy and grace of the Lord to cover them. One of the main tactics of satan is to get us to judge each other instead of praying for each other, so he can get at us to destroy us.

Chapter Fourteen

Prayer of Intercession For the Backslidden or Unsaved

When you are in the heavenly Courtroom, first you repent and asked forgiveness for your own sin. This is an important step. Then you are ready to stand in the gap and bring your petition before the Judge on behalf of a person or situation. You repent for their sins and ask for their forgiveness, and request that their case be moved from the Courtroom of Judgment to the Throne Room of Grace and Mercy.

If you are praying with the person, you can insert their name when you pray. If you are praying for someone who is not present, just make the adjustments to the wording. Once you have repented for your own sin, this is an example of how to pray, following the protocol of the heavenly Courtroom.

Dear Heavenly Father

_____ and I _____ are standing here today before You, (or I bring ____ before You) to repent on behalf of any sin that_____ has committed against you. We ask forgiveness for this sin.

We ask that you would move this case from the Courtroom of Judgment to the Throne Room of Grace and Mercy for a season of grace and mercy. Please remove the veil from the eyes of _____ understanding. I declare that _____ will see and embrace Your truth in their life.

Having repented and asked the Lord for forgiveness, and to move the case into His grace and mercy, be assured He will do it.

If we confess our sins, He is faithful and just to forgive us our sins and to cleanse us from all unrighteousness. (1 John 1:9)

Then you can decree these scriptures on behalf of the person or situation, inserting their name or 'him/her, his/hers as appropriate:

Plead ____ cause, O LORD, with those who strive with ____; fight against those who fight against ____. Take hold of shield and buckler and stand up for ____ help. Draw out the spear and stop those who pursue ____. Say to ____ soul, "I am your salvation."

____ soul shall be joyful in the Lord; ____ shall rejoice in His salvation; all ____ bones shall say, Lord, who is like unto You who delivered the poor from him that is too strong for him, yea the poor and the needy from him that triumphs over him. Keep ____ soul, and deliver ____; Let ____ not be ashamed, for ____ put ____ trust in You. Direct ____ footsteps according to your word; let no sin rule over ____.

____ waited patiently for the LORD; and God inclined His ear to ____, and heard ____ cry. He brought ____ up also out of a horrible pit, out of the miry clay, and set ____ feet upon a rock, and established ____ goings. And he has put a new song in ____ mouth, even praise to our God: many shall see it, and fear, and shall trust in the LORD. Then ____ said; behold ____ come, ____ delight to do thy will, O my God: yes, Your law is within ____ heart. I know your name and ____ will put ____ trust in You: for You, Lord, have not forsaken ____.

Lord, You say that You will pour water on him who is thirsty, and floods on the dry ground; You will pour Your Spirit on ____descendants, and Your blessings on ____ offspring; they will spring up among the grass like willows by the watercourses. One will say "I am the Lord's; another will call himself by the name of Jacob; another will write with his hand, "The Lord's", and name himself by the name of Jacob. You say, to ____ to refrain ____voice from weeping, and ____ eyes from tears for ____work will be rewarded, and ____ shall come again from the land of the enemy. You say there is hope in ____ end and that ____will come again to their own home. (Isaiah.44:3-5; Jeremiah 31:16-17)

Bless the LORD, O my soul; And all that is within me, bless His holy name! Bless the LORD, O my soul, And forget not all His benefits: Who forgives all ____ iniquities, Who heals all ____diseases, Who redeems ____ life from destruction, Who crowns ____ with loving kindness and tender mercies, Who satisfies ____ mouth with good things, So that ____youth is renewed like the eagle's. The LORD executes righteousness and justice for ____who is oppressed. They will decree Psalms 124:7 over themselves, 'I have escaped like a bird from the snare of the fowlers, the trap is broken and I have escaped!' (From Psalm 35:9-10,20; Psalm 25:20; Psalms 119:133; Psalm 35:1-3; Psalm 9:10; Psalm 40:1-3,7-8; Psalm 103:1-6)

If you are new to intercession, you should read and meditate on these scriptures so they become yours so you are not just reading my words. The prayers and decrees suggested in this book are guidelines. As you are reading, many other scriptures will speak to you about His protection. Take the promises of God and make them a part of your life. The Word brings life!

Write it down

Testimony used in an earthly courtroom is written, like a police report or a medical record. There is a saying in the medical field (and most likely other fields) that says, "If it isn't written, it didn't happen." Written history is a testimony.

When we make a decree, it is important to have it written down. *To make a decree* is to judge, to determine judicially; to resolve by sentence, to determine or resolve legislatively; a judicial decision or determination of a litigated case. *Litigate* means to bring before a court of law for a decision, contending in law. *(Webster's Encyclopedic Dictionary of the English Language 1984.)*

When we are quoting scripture, it is as if the Lord is speaking it thru us. If you have it written down, you will be able to remind Him of your prayers and petitions. When the enemy says to you, as he said to Eve in the garden, "Did God really say that?" you can reply, 'it is written'. If you have recorded the decrees from the Lord, you can always use this strategy against the accuser. And you get the benefit of reviewing the Word of the Lord over you.

A good attorney prepares before going into the courtroom. As my husband and I prepared our appeal in Stacie's case before the Lord, we were ready with the scriptures we had found and written down to decree over her. It was a joy to remind the Lord what He had said in His Word that He would do for her. We also wrote down praise scriptures to quote to the Lord.

Some people ask if we took Stacie's case into the Courtroom each time we prayed for her, or if we just quoted the scriptures. In our case, we did go back into the Courtroom to present our appeal several times, asking for her forgiveness. We quoted the promises in the scriptures He had given us, and we praised Him for the victory. I would suggest, since each case is different, ask the Lord what you are to do. It could be that taking them into the Courtroom once is sufficient.

And, as you pray, keep your Bible handy and paper and pen to write down anything the Holy Spirit may reveal to you about your case.

As I wrote down the dream about how to pray for my daughter, it became a testimony to the goodness of the Lord; then it turned into a book to help others. If I hadn't written the book, the Lord wouldn't be getting the glory He deserves for the miracle He performed for us. He wants to perform miracles for you too.

*Contend, Lord, with those
who contend with me;
fight against those who
fight against me.
Take up shield and armor;
arise and come to my aid.*
Psalm 35:1-2

Chapter Fifteen

Addressing the Accuser

After we have repented and been forgiven and moved from judgment into grace, we can and should address the accuser.

Why should we address our enemy? In the protocol of the Courtroom, this is the proper place to speak to the accuser. This is a safe place to confront the enemy because you have taken away his legal rights!

This is where we execute the judgment written upon him that that is referred to in Psalm 149:8,9. This could also be called contending prayer. As we address our accuser with scripture, we are describing what the Lord will do to our enemy as He contends on our behalf.

The Judge asks: "Is there anything you would like to say to your accuser?" We reply, "With all due respect, Your Honor, I will quote Your Word to him, which is highest praise to You and executes the judgment written upon him."

The Lord says that ___ adversaries shall be clothed with shame. You shall cover your own self with confusion as with a mantle. My Lord says in His Word that His hand shall find each and every one of ___ enemies, He shall make you as a fiery oven in the time of His anger He shall swallow you in His wrath, and His fire shall devour you. Your fruit shall be destroyed from the land and your bad seed from among the children of men.

You have intended evil against ____; you imagined a mischievous device which you are not able to perform. ____ Father will destroy your schemes and confuse your tongues. You shall be confounded and put to shame. You shall be turned back and brought to confusion because you have devised ____ hurt. You shall be as chaff before the wind and the angel of the Lord shall chase you. Your way will be dark and slippery and the angel of the Lord shall persecute you.

You have hid a net and dug for ___ soul. Destruction will come upon you unawares; and the net that you hid for ___ will catch you and into the destruction you planned for ___ you shall fall. (Psalm 109:29; Psalm 21:8-11; Psalm 35)

Chapter Sixteen

Praises

Bless the Lord with a thankful heart, knowing your petition has been heard. The Lord will move on your behalf as you praise Him with highest praises. Here are some of the praises I use when thanking the Lord.

Lord you have established your throne in heaven and Your kingdom rules over all. For You, Lord, are my Judge and Lawgiver, You are my King, You will save me. My soul shall be joyful in the You. I shall rejoice in Your salvation. Be exalted, O Lord, in Your own strength. I will sing and praise your great power.

Father, I thank You that you have not withheld Your great mercies from me. May Your loving kindness and truth continually preserve me. As the heaven is high above the earth, so great is your mercy toward one who fears You, for Your mercy is great above the heavens and Your truth reaches unto the clouds.

I will make a joyful noise to You and serve You with gladness. I will come before You with singing. Lord, You are my God. It is You who has made me. I enter Your gates with thanksgiving and come into Your courts with praise. Bless the Lord O my soul! You are very great, Lord. You are clothed with honor and majesty. You are covered with light as a garment.

Dear Jesus, thank You for Your loving sacrifice for me. You died so I could be free. I will strive, with the help of the Holy Spirit, to walk in love towards others as You loved me. I will not judge and I will extend mercy and grace as You extend mercy and grace to me daily. I ask that I could become more like You every day so that when others see me, they will see You. Help me to desire the meat of Your Word; as I read it, I will be washed clean. Teach me Your ways. Thank You, Lord, for listening and for helping me to walk deeper in faith and to be bolder in prayer.

Dear Holy Spirit, I thank You for Your presence on this earth. You surround me with Your presence; You inhabit my being. You comfort and encourage me during times of trouble in my life. You bring divine revelation to me as I need it; You bring all things to my remembrance. You reveal treasure hidden in deep places when I least expect it. Scriptures that I have read in the past but can't recall, You bring them to my mind. You have perfect recall and love to help me out, and I thank You for that. You are the light that is within me that casts out darkness. Thank You for lighting my path and divinely directing me every day. I bless you for all of those things that you do for me that I do not recognize, as You are working in my life. Amen. (Psalm 103:19; Isaiah 33:22; Psalm 35:4-9; Psalm 21:13; Psalm 40:11; Psalm 103:11; Psalm 108:4-5; Psalm 104:1)

Chapter Seventeen

Repent, Repent, Petition, Praise

Here is a review of the protocol for entering the Courtroom of Heaven, as given in the dream and validated by the Word of God.

As you are preparing to go into the Courtroom, and when you are praying in the Courtroom, listen for the Holy Spirit; He will help you to pray as you ought.

Repent, repent, petition, praise, declare

✷ Repent for your sins and ask the Judge to move you into the Throne Room of Grace and Mercy.

Don't skip this part. Ask the Holy Spirit to show you anything in your life that needs repentance and forgiveness. Remember, to repent means to change your ways. You may need to ask for His grace to be able to truly repent.

✷ Stand in the gap for the person/situation; repent on behalf of their sins that have given the enemy a legal right to work in their life. Chapter 14 has an example of this prayer.

Of course, God can't forgive the person just because you ask Him to, but it allows Him to move the person into His Throne Room of Grace and Mercy and work in the situation so that they will come to the truth and ask for forgiveness for themselves.

✱ Petition the Judge to move the case from the Courtroom of Judgment to the Throne Room of Grace and Mercy.

✱ Execute the judgment written against the accuser. DON'T do this unless you have followed the protocol above. See Chapter 15.

✱ Praise the Father, Son and Holy Spirit for the perfect resolution of your case. There are many scriptures you can use – some examples have been given in the Chapter 16.

✱ Once the case is settled in the Courtroom of Heaven, praise Him for the victory by continuing to decree what He has promised in His Word pertaining to your case. Use the decrees in Chapter 14, adding what the Holy Spirit may have given you for your particular prayer focus.

✱ And having done all, stand!!!

But thanks be to God! He gives us the victory through our Lord Jesus Christ. Therefore, my dear brothers and sisters, stand firm. Let nothing move you. Always give yourselves fully to the work of the Lord, because you know that your labor in the Lord is not in vain. —1 Corinthians 15:57-58 NIV

COMING SOON!

**Heavenly Advance
Prophetic Intercession
Activating the Forces of God's Angelic Armies**

This book describes what the term "prophetic intercession" means, and how it has played a significant role throughout history in changing the lives, communities, and the course of nations.

You will read examples of actions of prophetic intercession as performed by Jesus, His disciples and others. These symbolic actions, directed by God, mobilized the forces of angelic hosts to move on their behalf to see His purposes fulfilled on the earth.

If you haven't yet spoken or performed an action of prophetic intercession, this book will lead the way for you to enter and experience the Kingdom of God on the earth in a new way.

About the Author

Jeanette Strauss was commissioned by the Lord to write this book about His Courtroom in Heaven, after receiving an answer to a prayer through a dream and a divine visitation.

After the dream, and the results of obeying what the Lord said to do, she began to research and share the story with others, along with the scriptures that validated the dream. As they applied the information contained in this book, lives were transformed and many began to intercede with a new joy they had never had before.

Answers to prayers came in situations that had seemed impossible. Everyone who has heard this testimony and prayed in this way has seen results; they say they now feel like the Lord is in control and they are no longer being tormented. They rest in the knowledge that the Judge will handle their case. Jeanette doesn't mind in the least being transparent about the mistakes she has learned from during her 30+ years as an intercessor. She gladly shares her testimonies, praying they will be a blessing to others.

Jeanette is in active ministry. In 1997, she and her husband, Bud, founded and are the co-owners of Glorious Creations. Glorious Creations is a Worship and Praise adornment company. Jeanette is ordained as a minister through Gospel Crusade and has been in full time ministry since 1998. Jeanette and her husband are active members of New Heart Ministries in Coldwater, Michigan. She is a member of Aglow International and an intercessor for Southwest Michigan under the leadership of Barbara Yoder of Breakthrough Apostolic Ministries (BAM), and a member intercessor for Heartland Apostolic Prayer Network (HAPN) for Michigan under Anita Christopher.

Cover art by James Nesbit

Overseer of Prepare the Way Ministries International. James has been used by God to help prepare the way for the coming awakening in America through strategic level intercessory assignments. He has unique insight and understanding. Overseer of Mountain Alliance of Illinois, HAPN and RPN state coordinator for Illinois, and overseer for the region named Joy Number Nine, which includes the states of Missouri, Kentucky, Illinois, Indiana, Ohio, and Michigan.

James also has a strong prophetic art mantle resting upon his life. He believes prophetic artists have a Habakkuk 2:2 assignment to write the vision and make it plain so the body can quickly understand it and run with the word of the Lord. As the old saying goes, "A picture is worth a thousand words." Peter Wagner and Cindy Jacobs have proclaimed him one of the leading prophetic artists in the earth today. The Lord has seen fit to allow his artwork to be displayed in many nations throughout the earth. Visit the online gallery at www.jamesnart.com.

James says, "I married over my head." Anyone who meets his lovely wife Colleen would agree, and they have been blessed with a wonderful son Isaac who is now 17, 6'3" and growing. He can also be reached through www.ptwministries.com or nesb7@aol.com

Other resources from Jeanette Strauss
Heavenly Impact

Symbolic Praise, Worship, and Intercession
"On Earth As It Is In Heaven"

This book is a must read for those seeking a Biblical foundation for the use of symbolic tools of praise, worship and intercession. This information presents clear guidelines concerning their proper place and use.

Explore the Possibilities!
Heavenly Impact guides you through Bible history and explains the relevance of worship adornment as it identifies strategic value to worship. Scripture references reveal that our actions on earth truly do have a "Heavenly Impact". Tools covered: flags, billows, Mat-teh', shofar, streamers, tabrets, and veils, vocabulary of movement and Biblical color symbolism. Also available in Spanish. $14.00

Heavenly Impact
Teaching Bundle

We have had such a wonderful response to the *Heavenly Impact* book, a *Teachers Manual* and *Student Workbook* are now available for use in teaching Dance Ministry or Small Life Groups. The *Teachers Manual* includes Prophetic Activations and Exercises at the end of the chapters and different discussion topics. Each chapter includes the questions, along with the answers, for the teacher's convenience and references the page the answer is on in the *Heavenly Impact* book. The *Student Workbook* includes the questions, prophetic activations and exercises, and a section of biblical significance of colors. We also include a "Certificate Of Completion" suitable for framing.

Set includes one *Heavenly Impact*, one *Teachers Manual*, one *Student Manual*, and one Certificate of Completion. $40.00

Redeem Your Home

This book contains Biblical teaching about the necessity of spiritually cleansing your home, apartment or business. It includes step-by-step instructions with prayers to read that will insure the dedication of your home, apartment or business to the Lord. This insures the removal of any demonic presence that may be residing within it. Don't wait; set your home, apartment, business and family free today! $10.00

Redeem Your Home & Anointing Oil

This set includes one copy of Redeem Your Home, and a vial of oil. The oil is a combination of olive oil from Israel and a kosher wine, which serves as a symbol of the Blood of Christ as the sacrificial lamb.

This oil/wine combination is to be placed over the doorposts and lintels as a symbol of covenant, for all of the heavenly realm to see. This wine is appropriately named "Shalom", which makes a prophetic statement that your home and every room you anoint are under God's covenant protection.

The word *shalom* means "peace," which includes being safe in mind, body or estate. It speaks of a sense of completeness and inner tranquility; nothing missing, nothing broken. The common western definition of peace is the absence of conflict or war, and fits well with what we are using it for as we anoint our homes. In Israel today, when you greet someone or say goodbye, you say, 'Shalom.' You are literally saying, "May you be full of well-being" or, "May health and prosperity be upon you." A $20 value for $18.00.

From God's Hands To Your Land

The Bible establishes the spiritual relationship between God and His land. The Lord desires to pour out His blessings on your land, but scripture says that His blessings can be blocked.

The Lord, as the Owner of the original title deed of all real estate, gave us the responsibility to subdue and take dominion over the land. Included in this book are step-by-step instructions for the Restoration Ceremony, with prayers and decrees to recite as you reconcile and redeem your land that will ensure that His blessings will flow freely on your land with no hindrances. Also available in Spanish. $10.00

Bless Your Land Kit

This kit contains the items you will need for the Restoration Ceremony. It contains: 1 copy of the book, *From God's Hands to Your Land,* 4 communion cups with wafers, milk, honey, harvest seeds, consecration oil, a Title Deed. $20.00

From the Courtroom of Heaven
to the Throne Room of Grace and Mercy

As a born again Christian, I had never given the Courtroom of Heaven a thought. Then, in an answer to prayer for our daughter who was backslidden, the Lord gave me a dream that contained a strategy to use in heaven's Courtroom. As a result, she was set free and restored. Included is the strategy that can be used to win your specific petition in the Heavenly Court. This revised edition includes additional revelation from the Lord, and more testimonies to the goodness of God when we take our petitions to Him in His Courtroom. $14.00 Also available in Spanish, and as a CD.

From the Courtroom of Heaven
to the Throne Room of Grace and Mercy
Prayers and Petitions

This is a companion to the book *From the Courtroom of Heaven to the Throne Room of Grace and Mercy*. It contains examples of prayers and petitions you can use in the Courtroom. They are "Court ready" and can be read, word for word, by filling in the blank with the name of the people and situations you are praying for. These prayers are in addition to those included in *From the Courtroom of Heaven to the Throne Room of Grace and Mercy*. $13.00

From the Courtroom of Heaven
to the Throne Room of Grace and Mercy
Teaching Bundle

Everything you need to teach a small group study or class at church in one neat package. The Bundle includes one copy of the book "From the Courtroom of Heaven to the Throne of Grace and Mercy" and one of the companion *Prayer and Petition* book, along with a flash drive that includes a teaching outline to print, and a Power Point presentation. $50.00.

Additional Courtroom books can be purchased at a 20% discount when ordering this set. To get the discounted price, call to order, or email us at Jeanette@gloriouscreations.net.

Glorious Creations
1114 Robinson Road, Quincy, Michigan 49082
517-639-4395   www.gloriouscreations.net

ORDER FORM

Produce	Price	Quantity		Total
From God's Hand To Your Land	$10.00	x _____	=	_____
De las Manos de Dios a Tu Tierra	$10.00	x _____	=	_____
Bless Your Land Kit	$20.00	x _____	=	_____
Redeem Your Home	$10.00	x _____	=	_____
Redeem Your Home & Oil	$18.00	x _____	=	_____
From the Courtroom of Heaven	$14.00	x _____	=	_____
From the Courtroom of Heaven Prayers and Petitions	$13.00	x _____	=	_____
From the Courtroom of Heaven Teaching Bundle	$50.00	x _____	=	_____
Heavenly Impact	$14.00	x _____	=	_____
Impacto Divino	$14.00	x _____	=	_____
Heavenly Impact Teaching Bundle	$40.00	x _____	=	_____
Heavenly Impact Student Workbook	$13.00	x _____	=	_____

Total due for Product   _____

Shipping & Handling   _____

Total Amount Due   _____

Shipping & Handling:
0-$9.95 $ 4.00
$10 - $19.95 $ 6.00
$20.00 - $39.95 $ 8.00
$40.00 -$60.00 $10.00
We ship Priority Mail.

PRODUCTS AVAILABLE

- All types of Worship Flags for Praise
- Angel Wings
- Anointing Oils and Balm of Gilead
- Books
- Books By: Jeanette Strauss
- CD's and DVD's
- Children's Praise
- Christian Prophetic Art
- Dance Garments for Praise and Worship Dance
- Debi Woods Calligraphy
- Fabrics, Tinsel, Appliqués & More
- Fan Streamers
- Gift Certificates
- Glory Rings / Glory Wavers
- Jewelry
- Prayer Shawls & Judaica
- Reduced Priced Items
- Shofars, Ram Horns & Trumpets
- Streamers
- Sword
- Tabrets/Glory Hoops
- Tambourine
- Threshing Floor Prayer Mats
- Veils/Mantles
- Wall Hangings/Banners

Glorious Creations
1114 Robinson Road
Quincy, Michigan 49082
517-639-4395
www.gloriouscreations.net